THE KILLING AT
CROWSWOOD CASTLE

FRAN SMITH

HOG FEN

CHAPTER 1

CROWSWOOD CASTLE 1876

*A*part from the occasional dispute among ladies' maids, the hierarchy at Crowswood Castle was perfectly clear. At the top, Edmund Royston, 4th Earl of Mountfitchet, landowner, nobleman; at the bottom, Billy Wagstaff, orphan, kitchen boy, dogsbody.

It was Billy who found the dead lady.

Billy slept in the kitchen. His duty every morning, after raking the coals in the ovens back to life, was to carry two jugs of hot water up to the attics: one for the footmen; one for the maids. If Billy was late, the whole household was late, which was unthinkable. He could not tell the time, but he knew he must hurry when the kitchen clock chimed five times.

This particular morning (he remembered it in every detail thirty years later), he was hurrying the two enamel jugs across the hall towards the back stairs when he tripped. There should have been nothing there, but his foot was caught and he dived. The pair of jugs were loosed into flight then clattered and splattered with outrageous noise onto the flagstones.

I am in for a beating, was Billy's first thought. But then he looked at what had tripped him and saw it was the pale and delicate hand of a lady lying lifeless at the foot of the great stairs.

Billy wanted to cry. Cry because he was sorry for the poor lady looking at him with dead eyes and a kink in her neck that didn't belong. But also because the whipping for this would be a mighty one. They might send him back to the workhouse. Cook threatened it often enough. He'd done nothing bad, as far as he knew, but that rarely helped. A kitchen boy was always in the wrong.

When his ear was seized from behind and he felt himself pulled to his feet, with a kick to help him along, Billy accepted his fate, but was shocked to see the kick had been delivered by the Earl himself.

They had never met. The Earl had been pointed out to Billy from a distance, with warnings: *Keep out of His Lordship's way or you'll catch it, my lad!* Kitchen talk was often of the Master's cruelty, especially to Her Ladyship. *He didn't ought to speak to no-one that way. He's held his fist to her, Mr Wallace, I seen it with me own eyes.*

Wallace, the butler, would only tighten his mouth.

2

He, Cook and several other members of staff had been at the castle since before the Countess arrived. They had witnessed every detail of the five-year marriage between Lady Caroline, the new Countess, pretty, gentle, gullible Lady Caroline, and Edmund Mountfitchet. A marriage to which he brought the title, the land and the castle, but also bankruptcy, dissolution and depravity, and she brought innocence, perhaps even to the point of simple-mindedness, and a large inherited fortune.

The Earl was fifteen years older than his wife. He thought her timid and dull-witted. He liked girls with a bit of fun about them who showed more bosom and laughed loudly. He was happiest visiting racetracks and gambling dens with his gang of old university chums. He liked to stand everyone champagne at the Club before they had a flutter at the roulette tables. He was rarely at Crowswood, preferring an apartment in Hanover Square.

Lady Caroline, the Countess, grew paler, gentler and vaguer with each year that passed. She wept at first, and hid in her private rooms. When she refused food, doctors were called. They recommended fresh air. She did not have a strong mind, they said. In low voices they told the Earl that his wife showed signs of insanity. Bleeding might help, they said, or a trip somewhere. Perhaps if he were to take her to Rome or Paris?

The Earl could think of plenty of ladies he would

dearly like to take to Rome or Paris, but his wife was not among them. He bought her a thick-set Dartmoor pony called Magnet instead and went back to London.

The Countess was not generally interested in horses but she visited Magnet and fed him oats which he snuffled from her palm with a velvety nose. He had none of the highly strung nerviness of horses she had met before. He looked at her patiently with gentle long-lashed eyes. It was love. Magnet learnt to pull the little cart that had stood in the stables unused for years and Caroline learnt to drive it. They went out daily, disappearing for whole afternoons to trot the lanes and by-ways, a familiar sight to villagers in every direction. All of whom had their own ideas, fuelled by scraps of observation and gossip, about life at the castle. Most of them pitied the pale young woman who never smiled or stopped to pass the time of day. She was odd, poor thing. Not the full shilling. A bit touched in the head. But who could blame her with that wrong'un as a husband.

WHEN WILLIAM WAGSTAFF THOUGHT BACK, years later, to that morning, he was still not able to work out why the Master, having pulled him out of the way by his ear, forgot about him entirely. The only possible explanation was that a kitchen boy was too small and far too lowly to matter.

Billy ran, at first, to the kitchen to hide, but then crept back to see what would happen. Creeping about was one of his skills, as were spying and keeping things to himself. Such were the gifts of his own nature and workhouse life.

From behind a long-case clock, he watched as the Master stood over the dead lady. He was still except for his hands, one of which clenched and the other kept touching his chin and head. His face was grey. His clothes were creased as if he had slept in them. He looked this way and that, particularly up the staircase.

The servants would appear very soon. The Master must have known that. He ran to open a door in the panelling under the winding staircase. Then Billy watched as his master bent, and with difficulty lifted the dead lady in his arms and carried her the few steps into the cupboard. The lady's arm jutted out straight and stiff. It resisted the narrow doorway with a jerk that visited Billy in dreams for many years. Her head and neck did not behave as they should either. She wore a shiny blue dress, which rustled and trailed, but only one shoe.

Behind the tall clock, Billy pressed his hands over his mouth to stop a sob from giving him away. Was all this wrong? It seemed wrong. Or was this just how Earls behaved?

Billy had seen death before; a horse in the street, a tubercular old man in the workhouse, a litter of puppies drowned in the river. None had been treated with any great ceremony, but none had been thrown in a cupboard, either. People had taken their hats off and spoken in low voices around the old man, respectful. The farmer's wife said she'd bury the puppies when he told her. The memory of their poor little bodies made tears run between his fingers. He stiffened with fear as the Earl shut the panel door and swept a look around the hallway, glancing his way but seeing nothing before hurrying towards the back stairs, usually used by the servants.

He has gone for help, Billy imagined, though what help there could be for a dead lady in a cupboard, he wasn't sure. He didn't know who she was. Had never seen her. One of the company from the night before, he guessed. A trace of her floral perfume was still in the air.

There were always parties when the Master was at home. He brought London friends who drank and kept the servants up and running around at all hours of the night. Billy heard the complaints in the kitchen. Some of these London friends were ladies. The servants disapproved. Why they should save a special disapproval for the lady friends, he didn't really know. But they did. To Billy, the ladies glimpsed occasionally out of a window seemed colourful and happy. They brought laughter with them and music too, on occasion. He heard them sometimes in the distance singing round the piano, cheering and laughing. Cook said they weren't respectable songs, but Billy liked them. There was normally so little laughter and music in the castle. And the ladies were pretty. One once gave him sixpence and winked at him after he chased down her hat blown off in the wind. Sixpence! He still had it, shiny and silver, hidden.

Tucked in his corner, Billy was distracted by these racing thoughts, but snapped back to attention as the Earl reappeared carrying a large bunch of keys. He began sorting through them to find one to fit the cupboard door. It was not an easy task. He tried one key after another, hissing and cursing under his breath, fumbling and rattling the great keyring, until, on about the tenth attempt, one fitted and he turned it and locked the door.

At that moment, Wallace, the butler appeared, on his way to the kitchen. Billy could hear movement on the back stairs, too. The maids and footmen were coming down, ready to begin their morning's work.

'AH, WALLACE! THERE YOU ARE.' His lordship stepped out from under the great stone stairs and intercepted the butler. 'We shall not breakfast before ten. My guests had a late night. Tell the maids not to disturb anyone before nine.'

'Certainly, Sir,' said Wallace, who had been startled by his master's sudden appearance, but knew better than to show surprise.

'Tell someone to bring my horse. I shall ride out early.'

'Yes, sir.' Wallace hesitated, detained by a feeling that something was amiss.

'Immediately!'

'Yes, sir.' The butler moved off to the kitchen.

Mr Wallace will look for me, Billy thought. He'll want me to run to the stables with the message about the horse.

The Earl held the keys behind his back until Wallace had gone, then turned and strode away.

Billy heard his name called in the distance. He waited until the Master was out of sight, then scurried towards the back stairs after the butler. As he passed one of the great oak tables that stood around the walls, his eye was caught by a glimpse of blue. It was the dead lady's other shoe, wedged against a clawed table leg. He picked it up, thrust it under his jacket, and ran on, but as he did, he looked up and saw Lady Caroline silent and still at the turn of the great stairs above.

Later he wondered how long she had been there, but at the time he only ran to the kitchen where he suffered a mild cuff round the ear for not being quicker and was told to run to the stables.

For the rest of the day, Billy watched. The lady remained in the cupboard. The Earl rode out and was back in half an hour. Breakfast and lunch were served. The servants went about their usual duties. The Earl and his guests were as cheerful as before. They drank champagne and played billiards and cards.

Much later, when he tried the cupboard door, it was unlocked and there was nobody inside. All that remained was the sweet smell of flowers he connected with the silken folds of the lady's dress.

He was ten years old. If it had not been for the embroidered shoe he had tucked under the blanket he slept on, Billy could have believed there had never been a dead lady at the foot of the stairs that morning.

CHAPTER 2

CAMBRIDGE, 1907.

*T*he sound of the crash–a fearful grinding of metal on metal followed by a prolonged clang and smash of impact–was loud enough to stop people in the street. Everyone who heard it turned towards its source; the station.

Vita, who had been walking without paying much attention to where she was, was jerked from her thoughts back into the daily world. Automatically, she turned and hurried in that direction.

The 9.10 from King's Cross had simply not stopped. In the subsequent official report of the event, the stationmaster said it had approached the platform at a reasonable speed of 3 or 4 miles per hour, but at the point where it should have slowed and pulled in gently, it had simply continued its forward motion, the engine piling into the buffers, the four carriages behind the engine shunting together with enough force to hurl passengers–most of them standing ready to alight–to the floor.

According to the report, four passengers were injured, but only one, a lady, required treatment.

The lady concerned, reported by the Cambridge Daily News to be Spanish, but who was in fact Argentinian, may have required treatment, but she refused it. When the reporter from the Daily News asked her name, she hit him several times with her umbrella.

When Vita hurried onto the platform to offer first aid, she was directed towards a lady in a striking scarlet outfit sitting alone on a bench. The lady's equally striking hat, still on her head, had been badly crumpled by the impact. An artificial songbird and a lacework veil hung off the misshapen brim at odd angles. Anxious railway officials hovered nearby, but none dared approach because the lady was raging at them in such a torrent of Spanish.

No great expertise in the language was needed to work out that the Almighty and all his saints were being called upon to rain down revenge on the half-witted pet monkey of Satan who had been so stupid as to drive his train straight into a wall. He was unfit to drive a bucket into a well, and yet some gibbering fool had entrusted a train and members of the public to his unworthy hands. His mother's morals were remarked upon unfavourably. His father's heritage, she suggested, included hogs, curs and donkeys. As

all this outrage was expressed, the half-detached orna-
mental bird bounced and jerked in the air around
her hat.

Even without Spanish, Vita could tell this lady
was not likely to be an easy patient. She was holding
one ankle with both hands, and though clearly in pain,
continued to beat off anyone who approached.

'It is a foreign lady,' the station master remarked,
leading Vita over. 'She is not speaking in English. Her
injuries must be treated, and it is important that we
take her address. Perhaps you could persuade her,
Miss?'

Vita, completely at a loss as to how to deal with
such fury, stood within sight of the angry lady in red
and wondered how to proceed. The problem was
swiftly solved when the injured lady spoke. Her
English was accented, but perfect.

'You! Young lady! Come here. Sit.' She patted the
bench beside her. 'Listen,' she said. 'I must get to
Newmarket. I cannot be delayed. Is this clear? You
understand me?'

'Yes. I fear you may be injured, though.'

'That does not signify. It is not serious. A little
pain only. But I must get to Newmarket. I have
missed my connection because of this imbecile of a
train driver. How can I get there immediately?'

'A cab?' Vita suggested.

'How long will it take?'

'I'm not sure. Perhaps an hour?'

'An hour? This is too long! I have an appointment.'

'There might be another train. I don't know for sure.'

'Ask him, the fool in the uniform.'

The lady in the battered hat nodded towards the station master, still waiting at a careful distance. He confirmed that the next Newmarket train was not for more than an hour.

The lady flailed her arms in frustration. 'This famous city has only one train an hour to Newmarket, where the finest horses are sold? Why? Why is this?'

Vita was not qualified to answer. She said instead, 'It would be wise to allow someone to examine your ankle. It needs treatment.'

The suggestion was waved aside. 'It's nothing,' she said. 'Find me a cab.'

A porter was dispatched to hail one. The lady then attempted to stand, but fell back as soon as she put weight on the injured ankle. 'Aiee! Come. Help me walk.'

All objections were ignored, so Vita held the lady up on one side, with a brave station porter on the other, and hopping to avoid using the injured leg, she made her way outside and into a cab.

The station master, appalled at the lack of official record, hurried after them, saying, 'I must have the lady's name and address. For the inquiry. There's always an inquiry!'

'For pity's sake. My name is Consuela Ramirez de Navarro,' she said.

Vita wondered how he would manage the spelling of that name.

'And your address, Madam?' He was writing in a little notebook.

'Crowswood Castle.'

'And where's that?'

'The name is enough. The post will find it,' she said, waving him aside. 'And you. You know medicine?' She had turned her attention to Vita.

'A little,' Vita said.

'So, come with me.'

'Oh, but I…' Vita had not planned a trip to Newmarket.

'Come. You treat my leg on the way. You are safe. I will bring you back. Come. We must go. I cannot be late.'

Much to her own surprise, Vita climbed into the cab.

'GOOD HEAVENS! And where did she take you?'

'To a grand stable yard. She met a man who bred horses. They examined one or two. They had a short discussion, shook hands, and we came back again. She was buying one, I imagine. Or selling one.'

'Crowswood? Now why does that name ring a bell?'

Aunt Louisa, wearing her painting apron, was preparing a new canvas. The French windows to her studio looked out onto the sunlit winter garden. A few last roses were bright points among the bare trees.

'I'd never heard of it, but she expected everyone to know Crowswood.'

'She sounds rather eccentric.'

'She would like you to paint her portrait, by the way.'

'Oh, would she now? And what gave her that idea?'

'I mentioned your work. She seized the thought immediately. Apparently, there is a portrait in the castle that she wishes to replace. A large, and by her description, truly dreadful portrait of the previous owner.'

Louisa lifted the canvas from her easel and lay it to dry on a table. She wiped her hands on her apron. 'And how were the examination results, Dear? Weren't they due to go up outside the Senate House today?'

Vita walked over and stood looking out of the French windows. 'Yes,' she said. 'They were there.'

'It was not good news?'

'I failed physics.'

'Is that serious?'

'My name was right at the bottom of the list overall.'

'And the other papers?'

'A little better. I scraped a pass. Anatomy was better.'

'So, it was not a disastrous result?'

Vita sighed, watching the neighbour's cat roll and stretch in a patch of sun. 'It amounts to the barest possible pass. I shall have to re-take physics, if they will allow it. It means a great deal more study. I doubt if the college will consider me for medicine now.'

Her aunt had come to stand beside her by the window. 'I won't have you oppressed or overburdened. Not for the vacation. You have worked ceaselessly. Rest and recreation are what you need now.'

'A better education is what I need. Or better intellectual capacities. Or a better memory. Or the ability to stay up all night and immediately remember everything I read. I certainly need something I don't have.'

For a moment, they both watched the dappled sunlight filtering into the garden through the trees. 'Where is Crowswood? Did your exotic lady tell you?'

'She seemed to think Crowswood Castle, England, was perfectly sufficient as an address.'

'If it's the place I'm thinking of, it's somewhere in Norfolk, so not too far away. Perhaps we should visit.'

16

'I gave her one of your cards. She'll probably invite us.'

'I wouldn't mind a little Norfolk air. The coast is splendid up there. A breath of the sea would do us both good. Would you come? It might be an interesting diversion.'

'Interesting diversions are what landed me at the bottom of the results list, Aunt, I fear.'

'You can bring a pile of books.'

'You always say that.'

'She keeps horses, this Miss Navarro?'

'She breeds them. A certain breed–wonderful Argentinian horses, she said. I forget the name, but she hardly stopped talking about them all the way to Newmarket. They are strong, intelligent, hardy, far superior to any English animal, apparently.'

Louisa raised her eyebrows. 'I wonder what they said about *that* in Newmarket!'

It was as if, after that first meeting, Crowswood Castle had taken up residence in the very air of Cambridge. Never having heard the name mentioned before, Vita now came across it everywhere she went.

In the gymnasium where her brother taught, the university library, the tearooms and even at her tutor's house, the name of Crowswood seemed somehow to infiltrate the conversation.

'Isn't that the most haunted place in England?' Aloysius Derbyshire, the proprietor, asked when she called for her brother at the gymnasium. 'You're not thinking of staying there, I hope?'

'Why not? Ghosts! It's all nonsense,' Vita said.

'You don't believe in the supernatural?' Derbyshire was practicing with a broadsword, swirling it through the air above his head. 'You dismiss it all, just like that?'

'Of course.'

'Spirits? Fairies? Poltergeists? All nonsense?' He took a different stance and began slicing his invisible opponent in a figure of eight. 'You are a woman of steel, I must say. Nothing in the world would induce me to set foot in a place like Crowswood. I get the creeps locking up here at night!'

'I ONCE SAW ONE, YOU KNOW,' Miss Shorto remarked. They were sitting in her garden, very long and overgrown, in Hartford Street. Miss Shorto was now, in fact, Mrs Underhill, but Vita had not yet adapted to the new name.

'You saw a ghost?'

'I did. A grey lady. It was on Baker Street Undergound station.'

'What did she do?'

'She was just standing in the background, watching everybody come and go. Then she faded away.'

Vita took a slow sip of her tea, unsure how to react. Miss Shorto, one of her earliest tutors, represented the epitome of scientific learning and serious intellectual endeavour to Vita, and here she was talking about ghosts on the London Underground.

'Of course, there are plague pits all over London that were disturbed by the building of the underground railway lines,' Miss Shorto added. 'Mass burials. One imagines that if such a thing as ghosts existed, a place like that is where they would be. These shortbread biscuits are rather good. Do take one.'

IN THE UNIVERSITY LIBRARY, Vita took a seat at a table already piled with books and saw that the top one was entitled, 'The Scientific Investigation of Psychic Phenomena: a report of the Institute for Psychic and Supernatural Research.' She ignored it for twenty minutes, focusing successfully on her own work, but then found herself flicking through the table of contents, and came across Crowswood Castle: Unexplained Manifestations Observed by Reliable Witnesses over a Sustained Period. The castle, she read, had attracted researchers for many years because of the intensity of the unexplained phenomena reported. The author suggested that this was connected to the sad history of its owners.

IT CERTAINLY SEEMED AN UNLUCKY PLACE. Residents of the castle, when Vita glanced through the pages, made a general habit of meeting sudden, unhappy ends. They tumbled from battlements, contracted dread illnesses or died in duels and hunting accidents far more often than could reasonably be expected. One even fell from the basket of an early hot-air balloon, though that was seventy years before. The engraved image of Crowswood in C.L. Harris's Castles of England showed a lowering grey block of Norman origins closely surrounded by overgrown oaks. Dour was the word repeatedly used to describe it.

THE INVITATION, when it arrived, was accompanied by a substantial cheque: a payment in advance for even considering making a portrait. Miss Navarro understood that Mrs Brocklehurst was a sought-after portraitist. She asked no special favours, but if Mrs Brocklehurst would be gracious enough to visit, Miss Navarro felt certain they could come to some arrangement over the commission, even if it could not be executed until long into the future. Should this not prove possible, Miss Navarro would welcome the company of Mrs Brocklehurst and her niece anyway, in gratitude for the kindness Miss Carew had shown her at the time of the unfortunate accident at Cambridge station. Her home would be their home for as long as they cared to stay. She would send a carriage to collect them if they named a date.

Vita felt the elegance and old-fashioned formality of the letter was marvellously at odds with Miss Navarro's abrupt, not to say violent, behaviour in person at the time of the accident. The contradiction made her smile.

'How would you describe Miss Navarro's appearance, Dear?' Aunt Louisa asked, standing in the hall with the opened letter in her hand. 'And what is her age, would you say?'

Vita had a poor memory for clothing, but it was easy to remember Miss Navarro's scarlet outfit and battered fedora hat. 'She is probably in her forties,' she guessed. 'Dark and striking to look at. Beautiful in a proud way.'

'It would be rather agreeable to paint a lady,' Louisa said. 'Frankly, I am a little tired of beards. Oh, but please never repeat that to a gentleman.'

'Before you decide, Aunt, I should tell you what I've discovered about Crowswood Castle.'

'Is it cold?' asked Louisa. 'The food dreadful? The staff surly and dishonest? This is a large cheque.'

'It is famously haunted and riven with stories of gloom and ill fortune.'

'I see.' Aunt Louisa considered this information for a moment, then glanced again at the cheque. 'Are you discouraged by such stories, Dear?'

'Me? No, certainly not.'

'Good. Neither am I. Although, I suppose it is easy to be brave in one's own home on a bright morning. A gloomy castle's shadowy corners at midnight might test us a little.'

'They might.'

'Let's go and see. I'll write and suggest she sends her carriage on Tuesday.'

'I shall have to pack my books.'

'Of course. I shall ask Miss Navarro to provide a peaceful place for your studies when I accept the invitation.'

CHAPTER 4

$\mathcal{T}$he carriage that collected them from Eden Street was the grandest vehicle Vita and Louisa had ever ridden in. Its interior was quilted and plush and its springs efficient enough to make a long drive no hardship at all. They pulled into the woodland around Crowswood as dusk fell and, although the austere Norman profile of the castle was plain to see, its windows were lit and welcoming, and they were swiftly led in by willing staff, most of whom seemed to be Spanish-speakers.

The exception was the butler, who introduced himself as Wagstaff. 'Miss Navarro will join you shortly,' he said. 'She is settling the horses.'

The interior of Crowswood was not the gloomy ruin they had expected, either. The hall was freshly decorated. Vases of greenery brightened almost every surface and the furnishings and upholstery were colourful. Most appeared to be new. This was in dramatic contrast to other stately houses Louisa had visited, where the owners took a pride in inheriting their furniture in its entirety and disdained anything that was not antique on principle.

They were led by Wagstaff to a modestly sized but comfortable sitting room hung all about with paintings. Most were of beautiful horses. The exception, facing them from over the fireplace, was an unusual portrait of a pale lady in a silver grey gown.

'This is a curiosity,' Louisa said. They both stood looking up at the painting. 'Look at the frame, for one thing.'

All the other pictures around them were in ornate frames, richly gilded, but this portrait had only the plainest square strips of wood around it. The subject was a young woman, posed against a shadowy background. Large eyed and solemn, she directed a piercingly intense gaze out at the viewer. Two crows, one in a cage, one on a perch, also glared out on either side of her.

'You found the Countess, I see,' a voice declared behind them. Miss Navarro strode into the room. 'Excuse my clothing. My new horses arrived today. They are disturbed by the journey. It took us some time to settle them. Will you take some wine?'

Without waiting for an answer, she threw open a cabinet and poured three glasses, carrying them over to her guests herself and inviting them to sit before throwing herself onto a sofa. She wore loose trousers and a white shirt rolled at the sleeves and smudged with dirt. Her dark hair was pulled back from her face and plaited into a long braid that hung down her back. On her feet were soft woollen slippers in the form of boots.

'My house is informal. It is my habit,' she said. 'I should present myself. I am Consuela Ramirez de Navarro, from Argentina. Thank you for coming. I hope you will be comfortable. I know Miss Vita Carew, of course, and you,' she turned with a smile to Louisa, 'you must be her aunt. The painter of portraits.'

'I am. Louisa Brocklehurst. How do you do?'

'You are both most welcome. The maids will show you to your rooms soon, but I wanted you to see the Countess first. She is strange, no?'

'You wish to replace her, I gather,' Louisa said.

'I do. She has watched me for three years, since I arrived here, and, bluntly, I should like to be free of her now.'

'You would like your own portrait to replace her?'

'Exactly. It is a fitting end to the renovations. Although, in truth, repairs to an ancient place like this are endless. It is like casting one's fortune into a bottomless well!' With a gesture of cheerful resignation, Miss Navarro took a hearty swig of her wine. 'But we can discuss this further over dinner. You are tired, no doubt. I will have the maids show you to your rooms.'

'Your maids are Spanish?' Louisa asked.

'Argentinian. I brought most of my staff. Wagstaff and a few others in the kitchen and garden have been here at Crowswood for many years, but I brought my own household.'

Her guests looked surprised, but Miss Navarro only shrugged. 'I am alone. I have no family here, and very little left in Argentina either. My staff are dedicated and loyal. They have known me since I was born. They are like a family. Why would I leave them behind?'

And with this radical declaration, she rang the bell and a pair of maids appeared, ready to guide Vita and Louisa to their rooms.

'One more thing before you go. You probably know that this place has a certain reputation. It is thought to be full of spirits and all sorts of ghosts and other frightful presences.' She looked across at them seriously for a moment or two. 'Surprisingly few visitors are willing to spend the night, but I can assure you that in all the time I have lived in the castle, I have been troubled by nothing of that sort whatever. I take it you are not superstitious yourselves?'

'We are not,' Louisa said more firmly than Vita expected.

'Good. Then we shall change now for dinner. I prefer to dress informally, but ladies, you must feel free to suit yourselves. We dine at eight. It will be only the three of us tonight.'

THE ROOMS WERE UP two flights of worn stone steps. Vita wondered, as she climbed behind the maid, how many footsteps up and down it took to carve a smooth indentation into stone. Five hundred years of passing feet. She found the climb harder than usual and was left trailing behind her aunt. Her throat felt sore.

Their neighbouring bedrooms shared a single door into a small private lobby equipped, Vita was pleased to see, as a library with bookshelves and an armchair. From that, doors on either side led to the bedrooms. Vita followed the elegant young maid and found herself in a wood panelled room with cavernously vaulted ceilings. An enormous bed with dark carved pillars on each corner stood across the room from a vast stone fireplace.

The maid showed Vita where her clothes had been placed in an ancient carved armoire. She then opened another arched door in the panelling and displayed–of all wonders–an enormous private bathroom. A monster of a bath tub stood on clawed feet on a raised plinth in the centre of the room. One end of it was enclosed by a pillar box lined with elaborate brass pipework, so that a bather might stand and be sprayed from head to toe by fountains of water. The maid attempted to demonstrate its operation to Vita, but Vita could not follow.

Left alone, she sat in an armchair, suddenly lacking the energy even to explore. Her head was pounding.

'Vita? Are you ready, Dear?' Louisa, changed for dinner, had come in and found Vita asleep. 'Oh, you have not changed. You look flushed, Vita.' She put her hand to her niece's forehead. It felt hot. 'Are you unwell?'

'A headache and my throat is sore.'

'Not well enough for dinner?'

Vita shook her head. 'I couldn't eat.'

'Shall I help you into bed? Should we send for a doctor?'

'No, no,' Vita shook her head. 'I can put myself to bed.'

'Well, if you're sure. I shall ask them to send up some broth, perhaps.'

'Tea? I should like some tea for my throat.'

'Tea it is. I'm not happy to leave you feverish here alone. Perhaps I should make excuses for both of us?'

'No need. I shall just have an early night. You go and join Miss Navarro.'

Her aunt left, and Vita, now feeling heavy and slow in every limb, changed into her nightdress and sat again in the armchair, wrapped in a woollen blanket from the bed. Even the few steps to the little library to find a book were beyond her.

People came with tea. They helped her into bed. They arranged her bedcovers. Hands were pressed to her forehead. Low-voiced conversations took place. Sleep and darkness overcame her, broken by intervals of heat, thirst, and the awful rasping of her painful throat. There were dreams, too. Urgent dreams full of menace and complex contradictory instructions.

She woke once with her throat burning, reached for a glass of water, and found someone sitting by the bed; a lady she who seemed to be watching over her, helped her to drink and fetched more water from the bathroom to replenish the jug.

When she next grew too hot and threw aside the covers, the same quiet, grey-haired lady pressed a cool cloth to her forehead and straightened the tangled sheets. It was kind, Vita thought, the idea piercing a tangle of jumbled thoughts, for someone to have sent a nurse. Soon, even that thought was washed away by aches that spread to every joint. No position was comfortable, no relief could be found, except when hot and restless sleep pulled her in, clammy, and crowded with writhing dreams.

CHAPTER 5

'*I* t was all so long ago,' the lady beside the bed was saying. 'It feels as if my memories belonged to someone else.'

Lightning flashed beyond the curtains and in the silence before the thunder cracked, Vita could hear heavy rain thrashing against the windows.

'I was afraid of storms when I was young,' the lady said, looking toward the flickering windows. 'I was afraid of many things. Dogs, the dark, crows, the great dark trees. I knew from the first moment I saw it that I could never be happy here at Crowswood. All light and sunshine had been driven out of this place. It was all shadows.'

Vita's face felt hot, but she shivered as chills ran over her skin. Her eyes burned and felt gritty. She wanted to ask this nurse a question, but the effort required to do so seemed impossible. Nothing made sense. She gave up and drifted into sleep again, waking after what might have been five minutes or an hour to find the nurse speaking again.

'I should have told my father. But I was under his spell from the start. I was weak-willed. He told me what to do and what to think. I believed him.' She stood and adjusted Vita's pillows, putting the back of a cool hand to her cheek. 'Choose carefully when you marry, my dear. Be careful.'

'SHE IS BURNING WITH FEVER, STILL.' It was her aunt's voice. 'There are signs of delirium.'

'I shall send for the doctor. There is a man in the village. He has treated my staff.'

'You do not use him yourself?'

'I have had no cause. I am well, always, thank God.'

'WHERE IS THE OLD NURSE?' Vita tries to sit up, but it is too exhausting. Her voice is a hoarse whisper. Her throat has closed. She feels as if she has swallowed the blade of a sword.

'We have sent for the doctor, Vita.' Her aunt's face appears and then merges back into the darkness.

There is a loud ringing in Vita's ears. She grasps her aunt's hand.

'I must be cautious about who I marry,' she tries urgently to say. But only a husky groan emerges. She gives up and falls back into the hot pillow.

A VOICE she did not know then. A man's voice. In the background, speaking in low tones to the other people in the room. There is agreement. He steps to the bedside and holds her wrist to take a pulse. His fingers are light, cool.

'I am Doctor Haslam,' he says. 'I am going to listen to your heart and your breathing.'

Do what you like, Vita thinks. *I am busy sleeping.*

'Can you open your mouth, please, Miss Carew?'

It seems an unpleasant request. She is not sure the effort will be worth it.

'Come, I'll help you sit.'

Various arms pull her up.

'Now, open your mouth as wide as you can.'

She opens it, cold air rushes in and takes away her breath. She coughs and the throat seems to close entirely. He has slipped a wooden depressor into her mouth to hold her tongue. She can't breathe. Two others are holding her up and she jerks in their hands, struggling for air.

'I've seen enough,' he says. 'It is a severe throat

infection. Her tonsils are badly inflamed. The inflammation has not yet reached its peak. If it develops into a quinsy, I may need to operate to lance the swelling. It can be very serious.'

'When will you know?' The voice was Aunt Louisa's.

'I shall watch her tonight. It passes sometimes. She is young and generally in good health, would you say?'

'She is strong, but she has overworked for several years. It may have undermined her constitution.'

'How so?'

'She is a student. She was hoping to study medicine. She completed examinations recently. Not all were successful.'

He stepped back. His shirt sleeves were rolled. 'Well, that would be strain enough, I suppose,' he said, washing his hands in the bowl provided on the nightstand. 'For now, I shall give her this tincture to try to break the fever, and you will help me, please, to spoon it into her mouth.'

Vita heard some of this, feeling only a slight interest. She wanted to sleep in peace, if only the burning pain in her throat would allow it. Administering the medicine was another matter. She fought for breath; the doctor and his helpers fought to get a few drops of something that burned like acid into her throat.

The night wore on. Surfacing from a dream, Vita

knew there was a presence in the room. A shadow moved near the bedside. She knew she was not at home, but did not know where else she could be. She had a strong sense that she had fallen behind with something. She had work to catch up with, but only a slight idea of what the work might be. Books were involved. In one dream, she needed to build a staircase out of them in order to escape from an overheated library, but they were heavy and uncooperative and she kept slipping back.

By the morning, the illness had changed its form and focused its malevolence on her throat to the point where she could not speak or swallow. Propped up, she could breathe and sleep a little, but everything was hard work.

The doctor declared the operation on the tonsils would have to go ahead. He came with a colleague, laid sheets around Vita and trays of instruments in bowls. She recognised these instruments as if from somewhere very far away and long ago. A scalpel, a clamp, a swab. She felt a sudden dread–they were going to do something to her throat–but had not the strength or the understanding to resist. It must happen, whatever it was, whoever these people were. She was far too busy breathing to devote much energy to their activities.

From there it was a blurred but horrible confusion. Mouth forced open. Cold steel instrument against her tongue. Can't breathe. Hands holding her tightly down on every side. Holding her head still at an angle that made the pain of the throat unbearable. Can't breathe. Can't breathe. Sharp pain. The taste of blood, of something rank and foul. At one moment, she was drowning in it. Then it was over. She was propped upright. Hands touching her forehead, instruments listening at her chest, the murmur of conversation in the room. It was calmer now.

'She must be watched. The worst should be over now that it is drained.'

THE ROOM IS CALM LATER. She wakes, and it is light enough to make out the slumped figure of a young man in an armchair by the fire. He is formally dressed, but snoring. She tries to reach a glass of water on the nightstand, but cannot. Her throat is so sore it brings tears to her eyes, but she is also agonisingly thirsty. She stretches again for the glass, and this time knocks it onto the flagstone floor, where is shatters, causing the sleeping young man to rouse, but only slowly. He rubs his eyes and looks confused. He has forgotten where he is. Then it comes back to him, and he springs up and begins to fuss over the broken glass. He picks the larger pieces up, and then looks helplessly around, not knowing what to do with them, opting eventually for placing them in a watery pile on the great oak chest at the foot of the bed. Many of the shards are sharp and small, but the young man devotes himself to their collection, making many trips back and forth. At least once, he jerks, shakes his hand, and sucks a finger as if he has cut himself.

Vita watches all this and in her half-awake state finds his diligent application to such a task both foolish and peculiarly touching.

But she needs water. She tries to tell him, but no sound can be made from this throat filled with hot coals, so she raises her arm. He sees this from the foot of the bed and has to shake sharp pieces of broken glass from his wet fingers before he can come to the bedside. Vita touches her throat.

'Ah yes,' he says. 'Water.' He reaches for the carafe but, of course, there is no glass, so he puts it down again and hurries to the bathroom, returning with another. He fills it and holds it to her lips. The lovely water enters her mouth, but then has nowhere to go. Her throat is closed.

'It will be difficult at first, but you can swallow,' he says.

Vita thinks that is all very well for him to say. It is not his throat that is blocked forever with molten lava.

'Take a little. Just a little.'

Water is now spilling down her chin. She wants to cough, which she is fairly sure would explode her throat and kill her outright.

'Slowly,' he says. 'A drop at a time. Your throat is

damaged. This water will help, but you must take it slowly.'

Finally, a drop or two of lava burn and slice their way down. Once the immediate pain subsides, there is a little relief.

'I am Doctor Bennett. You must not try to talk. You have had surgery on your throat.'

He looks very young, this Doctor Bennett, Vita thinks. Five years her senior at best. She hopes he knows what he is doing. There is still a puddle of water where it has spilled on the floor. He is certainly not very good at clearing up. He takes her pulse and her temperature and writes both in a small notebook, treading spilled water round the room on his boots as he does so.

A nurse would know better, Vita thought. Where is the nurse?

'Your fever is passing, which is good. You will take water as often as possible today. Tomorrow a little broth, perhaps. We shall see. The maids will be here soon. I shall instruct them to help you drink. With luck, the worst is over now. Do not leave this bed. You must have complete rest.'

He walks away. She watches him pack his note-book into a black bag and fasten it. His long hair falls forward and has to be pushed back. His suit is rumpled. He has an old-fashioned look, she thinks, as if he inherited his grandfather's clothing. He runs his hand over his chin, feeling the stubble, picks up the bag and leaves the room, saying, 'The maids will be here soon, Miss Dean. I shall call in later.'

Miss Dean?

CHAPTER 6

'Three nights?' Vita wanted to say. But she could not speak, so all she could do was to look at her aunt in confusion.

'Yes, you have been in a fever. Delirious!' said her aunt, 'talking and thrashing about. You had us worried, my dear, I can tell you. I have written to your father and brother. I shall let them know of your improvement today. They will be enormously relieved. As am I.'

Her aunt stopped adjusting Vita's pillows and blankets and sat down at the bedside. 'Dr Haslam has been marvellous. He is only the local man, but thank heavens, he is a qualified surgeon. I dread to think what might have happened without him. Now you will be in some discomfort, Dear, I know, but his orders were strict. No activity of any sort. Not even reading. And speech is absolutely forbidden because the throat must be given time to recover. Without the proper rest, you could loose your voice permanently. Haslam says you may have paper and pencil tomorrow, but for the rest of today you must simply lie here with the curtains drawn and put all your strength into recovering.'

One of the Argentinian maids came in, bringing fresh drinking water and a bunch of dried flowers and myrtle leaves, which she arranged on a side table. She poured a little of the water for Vita, and left quietly.

'I have grown fond of Consuela's maids since you have been so ill,' Louisa remarked. 'They have been extremely kind. As has their mistress. We have spent a lot of time together. I have come to know Consuela quite well, I think. It's quite a story, but for another occasion, when you're stronger. I'll leave you now. Rest, Vita. Ring the bell if you need anything.'

With the curtains drawn, the day of intermittent sleep soon faded into night again. Her throat was parched and sharply painful, but she could manage to swallow a few drops of water. Kind maids came with sponges and towels and bathed her, speaking reassuringly in gentle Spanish. Doctor Haslam came and took her pulse and temperature. He looked in her eyes and persuaded her to open her mouth (an effort of extreme discomfort) so that the scarred tonsils could be seen. Vita choked until tears ran down her cheeks. She was left gasping and exhausted.

41

'Apologies, but it must be done,' Haslam said, patting her arm.

She wondered about Dr Haslam and how he came to be doctoring in remote Norfolk. How he trained in surgery. Where had he studied? What were his other patients like? Did he enjoy the work? What was his connection with the younger man – was Bennett a junior colleague? But speech was not allowed, so she could only store the questions.

The same questions were in her head later, when she woke and saw young Dr Bennett back in the chair by the fire. He was half turned away from her, holding his hands to the flames, rubbing them together as if they were frozen. The room seemed warm to Vita. All she could do was to watch from her pillows. His dark brown hair was long and wavy, falling over his collar. The front fell forward so that he swatted it back with his fingers in a habitual gesture. He had a short moustache, which compared to his hair was inclined to be ginger. It curled over his upper lip. It was the kind of moustache a young man might grow when he wanted to appear mature, perhaps. Otherwise he was clean shaven. His suit was dark, his waistcoat had place for six buttons but one, the fourth from the top, was missing.

Either he is married to a careless wife, Vita thought, drifting into sleep again, *or he has a forgetful housekeeper.*

Later, when she woke again and was not sure if it

was night or day, she realised the doctor's waistcoat button might be missing because he had slept in that chair over there for several nights in a row, and thus escaped the attentions of either wife or housekeeper. He had a serious face, she thought. And surprisingly pale blue eyes.

The night nurse was in the room again when she woke a little later.

'I did not mean to wake you,' the lady in grey said. 'I mean no harm. I only look in.'

She drifted into the chair beside the bed, her pale hands smoothing the sheet. 'The rooms are so pretty now. So bright. Such an improvement. I could never have imagined it. Everything was dark and gloomy when I was younger. Or perhaps it only seemed so to me. Unhappy memories are all I have of this place. He told me there were ghosts. The spirits of lost children. My mistake was always to believe what he told me. I was young, you see.'

Vita, barely awake, could not make sense of anything she said, but was drawn to the fluttery bird-like woman's gentle voice.

'He put thoughts into my head. I was not strong enough to resist them. I know that now. There. I won't trouble you further, my dear. I only wanted to see for myself that you were better. I'll say goodbye.'

And she drifted away.

This is a strange kind of nurse, Vita thought. But

so many things had been strange recently that she felt no great concern as sleep engulfed her again.

~

MISS NAVARRO VISITED the following day with a maid carrying soup.

'So!' she said, 'my guest is a little better! My cook has made a beef broth. In Argentina, we believe it cures everything. I know it will not be easy, but if you can swallow a little, it will richly reward the effort.'

'Did you know she is a genius, your aunt? Already she has begun the portrait and it will be magnificent. She does not allow me to see it, but I know it will be marvellous. It is vain, I suppose, to have my portrait made, but long ago I stopped to think of such things. I sit for only one hour a day because–oh, there is so much to do. My little horses are making an impression. People want to buy them. They want my stallions for their bloodlines. Do you know horses, Vita?'

Vita shook her head.

'Well, when you are well, I shall show you my *Criollos*. I have a breeding herd here now. Fine, fine animals: beautiful, strong, hardy, intelligent. I train them as no-one else can, but more than that, I know them. I know their hearts. I understand them. *Criollos*, they are loyal. They will run all night and day for an owner they trust. They will run until they die in harness, if a beloved owner asks it of them. I have known it. People love them here–you know what for? Polo ponies! They can turn like a ballet dancer. They are fast and fearless, too. Champions, every one!'

She stopped for a moment and took stock of where she was. 'Oh, I speak too much of my horses. I love them. Excuse me.'

Vita was smiling at her hostess's enthusiasm. Consuela's English was perfect. Her origins showed only in a few quirks of pronunciation, most noticeably a very charming way of saying 's'. It was nearly, but not quite, a lisp. The soup smelt delicious, but there seemed little hope of swallowing any, since someone had welded her throat permanently closed.

'I leave you to eat now, my dear guest. Take a little of this soup if you possibly can. Maria will help you. Oh, and the doctor says you may have this.'

She dropped a notebook and pencil on the bed as she left.

CHAPTER 7

*V*ita had a hundred questions she wanted to write, but first there was the soup to be dealt with.

Maria spread a napkin on the patient's chest and offered a spoonful with an encouraging smile. The rich beef stock wafted hints of herbs and onion, as well as its own deep meaty flavour under her nose, but Vita's throat said firmly, *no*. With no English for persuasion, Maria looked puzzled at Vita's refusal, then held up her hand to signal, ' Wait! I have an idea', and demonstrated the action of taking another, but this time much smaller spoonful. It was barely a few drops that she tendered this time.

Vita was overtaken by a spasm of coughing which tore at the inside of her throat and left her pale and breathless.

Once she had recovered, they both looked at the

steaming bowl of broth again, completely at a loss. Vita then seized the pencil and drew a teacup.

Understanding immediately, Maria fetched a cup and handed it to Vita with a little of the soup poured into it. Vita warily lifted the cup to her lips and allowed a mere drop to run down her throat, bracing herself against the rasping pain. The tiny amount found its way past the sore and swollen tonsils. It hurt, but it passed through. Both Maria and the patient felt a step forward had been taken, even if almost all the broth was subsequently taken away.

They were congratulating themselves quietly when they both heard a distant shout. It came from somewhere off in the gardens. It was sudden enough to draw Maria to the window, but she seemed unable to trace it.

After the maid had gone, Vita listened again, and heard footsteps on the stairs, movements outside and a general hubbub somewhere distant in the castle. It was late afternoon, and almost dark outside. She wondered about looking out of the window herself, but the effort of rising from the bed and walking all the way across the room seemed far too daunting. She felt feverish again, and lay back on her pillows, shivering and defeated.

HASLAM, when he called on the patient later, was business-like.

'I heard you took a little soup earlier,' he remarked, as he held her wrist in one hand and his fob watch in the other, timing her pulse.

She nodded.

'But only a little.' He dropped her wrist and turned to write the figure into her notes. He was left-handed, she noticed. 'I recommend honey dissolved in warm water and a poultice. They are already preparing the poultice downstairs. It should help to draw out the infection.'

She nodded again. He noted that her notebook had not been used except to draw a teacup. The observation made him narrow his eyes.

'How do you feel today?'

Lacking the energy to write anything, Vita only shrugged.

'I'd hoped you would be feeling a little stronger by today, but we must be patient. You have suffered a severe infection. It has inevitably taken its toll on your general strength and condition. Have you often suffered infections, Miss Carew?'

She shook her head.

'You are normally healthy, would you say?'

A nod.

'Well, then you can expect to regain your strength in a few days. But we must be vigilant. The fever must not be allowed to return.'

She suddenly felt no interest at all in Dr Haslam or her own illness and wanted only to rest. The room was growing dark. She wanted the exhausting day over.

He reached over and placed the cold glass stick of a thermometer under her tongue. When he withdrew it and wrote in the notes, she saw him shake his head. He was dissatisfied. His patient was not recovering as she should.

When Vita next opened her eyes, she could hear Dr Haslam speaking in a low voice, and was surprised to find that her aunt and Miss Navarro were back in the room.

'The fever is returning, I'm afraid,' the doctor told them. 'I am not content to leave her overnight.'

'One of my maids, perhaps?' Consuela suggested.

'I prefer to stay myself, as before. I shall be comfortable in the chair.'

'Can you tell why the fever might be returning?' Louisa asked, her voice anxious.

Haslam shook his head. 'It subsided immediately after the operation, which suggests that...'

They were interrupted by a clatter of boots and raised voices in the corridor outside. Someone knocked urgently on the door.

'Yes?' Consuela called.

The door opened to reveal Wagstaff, the butler, with several other men.

'I apologise, Madam, but there is an urgent matter needing your attention.'

'Miss Carew is unwell. This also is an urgent matter, as you well know,' she told him, irritated. 'Why do you interrupt?'

'Perhaps we could speak privately, Madam?'

She dismissed this request with a flick of her wrist. 'Just tell me now, Wagstaff, if the matter is so very urgent.'

Wagstaff looked pained. He glanced at the men–three or four workmen in boots, carrying their hats in their hands–in the passageway behind him. All looked back anxiously.

'Speak, Wagstaff! What is the matter?'

'Madam, the men have found something which they believe might be human remains. They were digging in the far corner of the garden and they came across a pile of old clothes. But when they looked more closely, it wasn't just clothing, it was a human body–or what remained of one–still dressed.'

'*Madre de dios!*' Consuela declared. 'What is this? Let me talk to the foreman.'

One of the workers, a grey-haired man with the mud still on his work clothes, stepped forward. He held a battered felt hat, working it in his hands as he spoke.

'We was in the far corner of the garden, Madam. We knew there was brickwork there, but we couldn't make out what it was. We thought it was a cistern or drain. One side was broken by tree roots. We could see a hollow, so we broke in. It's an old ice house. Domed brickwork buried underground. We found the body in there.'

'What did you do with it?' she asked.

'We had a look. Careful, like. It looked like a few rags, but when we looked more closely, it was easy enough to see that it was a dead body.'

'But why is it there? How is it there?' asked Miss Navarro.

The man looked at her blankly. He did not seem to understand the question. Then he added, 'It's old, Madam. It's been there a long time. There's not much of it left. Rotted, I'd say.'

'Perhaps I can be of some help?' Haslam interrupted, stepping forward. 'There are formalities in such an eventuality. The coroner will have to be notified, and so on. I could look at the body, if that would be helpful.'

'Oh, please, yes,' Miss Navarro grasped his arm in gratitude. 'I would be most grateful. And you men,' she gestured towards Wagstaff and the workers standing behind him. 'Show the doctor to the place.'

'Shall we move it, Madam?' the foreman asked her.

She looked uncertainly back at Haslam, who hesitated.

Vita, who had heard the conversation, roused herself for the first time, struggled to reach the pencil on her nightstand, and wrote something in the note-book. She held it towards Haslam. He read the scrawled words: *you must see it just as they found it.*

Haslam read it, but looked doubtful.

'Vita knows something about these matters, Dr Haslam,' Aunt Louisa told him. 'She works in the Police Surgeon's laboratory, if you recall.'

'Ah, yes,' he said.

Vita wrote something else and held it out. He read, *Very imp. Note every detail of place and position, etc.*

Haslam indicated that he understood this. 'I'll come and look now,' he told the men.

Vita nodded and pointed insistently at the message again. He thought she looked flushed.

'Yes. I understand,' he told her. 'I shall return as soon as I can.'

'I shall accompany,' Consuela said.

'As you wish,' Haslam replied. 'Perhaps a little tea meanwhile for Miss Carew? Will you stay with the patient, Mrs Brocklehurst?'

'Of course,' said her aunt.

When everyone else had left, Aunt Louisa patted her niece's hand. 'Well,' she said, 'I hope a mystery is not too much for you in your present condition, Vita, Dear.'

Vita, lying back on her pillows, managed a smile.

CHAPTER 8

he poultice, a hot strip of muslin spread with a concoction of menthol, oats and goose fat, kept everyone busy for the evening. The menthol made Vita's eyes water so much that she could not see, and the heat scalded her throat on the outside. But Dr Haslam and his helpers seemed to place great faith in the treatment.

Drowsing afterwards, Vita only dimly remembered the talk of the body being found. She tried to think about it, but could not focus her thoughts. The grey night nurse came into the room, but only to place a cool hand on her forehead and leave immediately.

There was a strangeness in the atmosphere, something different, Vita thought. She could suddenly smell the scent of some flowers Maria had brought to the room. Or perhaps that was a dream, too. It was difficult to know. At one moment during the darkest hours of the night, she thought she heard the door creak open and a figure move stealthily across the room. She took it to be Dr Bennett returning, but was then surprised to see the doctor's silhouette already slumped asleep in the armchair. The other figure–too small, on second thoughts, to be a grown man–paused and seemed to study the sleeping doctor before re-crossing the room and leaving as it had come in, closing the door with its characteristic creak as it left. It showed no interest in Vita, and didn't return.

Vita was feverish again. She reached for some water, but hadn't the strength to hold the cup. A dream came, in which she had her voice and could ride her bicycle to the examination hall, but could not make anyone listen to her.

'Miss Carew?'

A row of black-robed examiners looked stern and shook their heads. Her task was to explain the anatomy of the throat and she had studied the subject well, but when the grey-faced examiners asked a question, the sounds her voice made were not speech.

'Vita?'

They could not understand. 'Unfortunately,' they told her, 'you have failed.'

'No!' she wanted to plead with them. 'If you would listen, I know this, I can answer!'

But no sound came when she tried to speak.

'Vita?'

One of the examiners, with a kindly expression,

took her hand and held it to his lips as if to kiss it, but suddenly bit it instead.

The shock of it shuddered her awake. She opened her eyes to find Dr Haslam's hand on her shoulder. There were candles in the room. People in nightgowns.

'Your fever is too high, Vita. We must cool you.'

'I know the anatomy of the throat so well,' she told him, but it sounded like a long groan.

Maids pulled back the covers and laid damp towels over her. They sponged her face and hands with cool rosewater and the two of them fanned her with lacy fans. She wondered where the grey nurse was. Sleeping perhaps. Sleeping. It seemed an attractive idea, but where was her bicycle? She must remember to ask.

Dr Haslam was among several people in the room the next time she opened her eyes. He came over as she woke.

'I must examine the site of the operation, Miss Carew,' he said. 'It may be uncomfortable. It will help if you do not resist. I shall be as quick as I can.'

They piled pillows behind her and sat her up against them. Hands on all sides held her arms and legs down and grasped her head. She could not move. The doctor pulled open her jaw and pushed a cold clamp inside her mouth to hold it. She squirmed, instinctively twisting away from the pain. The hands around her tightened.

Bending close, Haslam thrust his flat spatula into the back of Vita's throat. Someone held a lamp so that he could see inside. Vita gasped, gagged, coughed, gurgled. Her feet tried to kick, her arms to fight them off. The doctor seemed to be choking her with a red-hot coal while a roomful of people looked on.

When it was over, Haslam went outside. Aunt Louisa pressed forward and took Vita's hand. There were tears in her aunt's eyes. Vita wished she could reassure her. 'You don't need to worry, Aunt,' she tried to say. 'The throat's anatomy is complicated. I will try harder. I think I can pass the examination, if only I study a little more.'

PROBLEMS. Such a series of complex problems to be solved. And so very tiring. Breathing itself asked such a lot. Forcing air past a furnace of a throat was hard labour. Water might help, but drinking required a dozen difficult and exhausting manoeuvres. It hardly seemed worthwhile. People were kind.

It was puzzling to find her brother and father in the room. She wanted to explain to them about the examination, so that they were not too disappointed. *I should have tried harder.*

Obviously it had been a foolish idea to study–she could not remember what it was she had been studying–throats? fevers? swallowing?–at the university. It all seemed so long ago.

I shall die now, I suppose, she thought. *I hope they will forgive me. Breathing is such hard work. I shall stop struggling now and rest.*

Peace. Silence. Drifting away.

But then, 'Oh no, Dear, it is never as simple as that. There is a time, but you must wait for it.'

The night nurse in grey sat stroking Vita's hand in the dark. 'It all comes right in the end,' she said. 'But you have to be patient and wait for the right time, the right people.'

Vita's throat, though aching and still raw, had loosened its vice-like grip on her windpipe. She was surprised to find herself breathing without the exhausting effort it had required before.

'I myself have waited a very long time,' the lady went on, 'but now at last he is found. They said he had gone to France, you know. And, of course, I was gone to Garston Lacey by then. The lawyers did all that. The lawyers and the London doctors.'

Vita listened without trying to make sense of these ramblings. They flowed over her awareness without making much impression. Like listening to a fairy tale in a language only partly understood.

'Oh, I thought it was the end of the world at first,' the old lady continued. 'I thought he had sent me to a prison. I truly thought I should die. If loneliness and fear alone could have killed me, I should have died in the first week. But the doctor who ran it was kind. The grounds were large. I was free to leave my room. I made friends. They were patients like me. We had all found a refuge, you see. There were limitations, but few of us felt the need to travel. Wagstaff even brought my little pony to be there with me. In good weather, I still went out driving. And there was nothing to fear when I returned. I soon made friends with Seraphina and then her brother, Joseph. Seraphina played the piano and Joseph painted beautifully. He painted my portrait.'

The lady's hands were delicate. She smoothed Vita's pillow.

'I shall not trouble you longer, now, Dear. I know you are still unwell. I wanted you to know. You can explain it to the others. I have never been good at explaining.'

Vita looked directly at her. She was the palest woman Vita had ever seen. Her skin was pearly, but eyes were large and dark. The front of her hair was white with traces of brown in the bun behind her head. But for the tracery of blue veins Vita could see beneath the frail skin at her neck, she seemed almost transparent. She smiled back, an unfocused movement of barely coloured lips.

'They have found him, you see, Dear. The Earl. My husband. In the ice house. He had gone away to France, they thought. He often went away. Nobody even told me at first. Later, there were papers and lawyers because of all the land and the castle standing empty. Was it mine? Was I competent? I didn't care. I had only ever been unhappy at Crowswood. I had no wish to return. But others cared. It took a long time, but in the end they found the Argentinian family.'

She pulled a shawl around her shoulders. 'I shall leave you to rest, but if I might ask a favour, Dear, could you tell them it is the Earl? It is he. It must be. Nobody listens to me, which is only to be expected. But they will listen to you. It should not be difficult to prove. He always wore a signet ring with an evil-looking bird on it. He liked such things. A crow from Crowswood, you see.'

She paused and added sadly, 'I wanted so much to please him. That is always a mistake, but you are wise enough to know that. I'll leave you now.'

And she left Vita staring into the darkness of the room, wondering if what she had just heard made any sort of sense.

*a*s dawn came, Vita slowly made out the sleeping figure of her brother in the armchair.

She watched him asleep for a while, then grew impatient and slapped one of her hands on the bed. He leapt to the bedside and put a hand to her forehead. 'Vita! How are you feeling now?' he said. 'Don't speak! You mustn't yet. Just nod.'

She did.

He looked delighted. 'The throat?'

She made a face and pointed to the water jug.

'Of course.' He filled a glass.

She found she could even swallow, if she was careful. The luxury! She picked up the notepad on her bed and wrote *how long?*

'How long have father and I been here? Three days. Aunt Louisa sent for us on Thursday. It took father a day to reach Cambridge, and we came on together from there. You have been ill for a week in all. They operated five days ago. It worked at first, but the fever did not go as Dr Haslam had expected. You have been very ill, Sis. We worried it was a secondary infection. He's been very good. He's visited every day.'

Vita took the pad again. *I failed physics*, she wrote.

Edward read the note and laughed. 'The paper can be taken again. Some of the chaps in my second year took it three or four times. Now, could you eat something? Haslam suggested soup or custard at first.'

'Did they find a body?' Vita wrote. 'I've had some very strange dreams.'

Edward looked wary. 'You should eat. Build up your strength a little before you start thinking about anything like that.'

'But did they?' she wrote.

He gave an exaggerated sigh and said, 'Yes. If you must know, workmen digging in the garden came across a body in an old brick ice house everyone had forgotten. Been there for years, or so they say. They've called the police in, but they haven't sent anyone yet.'

Is there a ring? Vita scrawled this and held the pad out impatiently for Edward to read.

'A ring?' he asked.

Was the body wearing a ring? Vita wrote. Impatience and weakness made her writing spiked and crooked on the page.

'Good Lord, I don't know. I'm keeping well away from all that. This place is creepy enough as it is. Pa saw a ghostly old lady creeping along a corridor last night, and I was kept awake half the night by a banging that sounded as if someone was knocking persistently at a distant door. This part of the castle is fine during the hours of daylight. Miss Navarro–she must have the heart of a lion, incidentally, to live here alone–has made a fine job of cheering the place up. But it's another matter after dark. After dark, it's all flitting shadows and sudden chills. Father has resorted to prayer, and I have turned to brandy, I'm afraid. But it's worth it to see you looking better. I shall let Aunt Louisa know immediately. Shall I have them send up some food?'

His sister nodded, but looked unenthusiastic.

'Custard or broth?' Edward asked.

Either, Vita wrote.

'I'll say both,' he told her. 'I'll finish anything you can't manage.'

Vita would have laughed if her throat had allowed it. It would clearly take more than a few hauntings to quell her brother's appetite.

'OH, MY DEAR GIRL!' the Reverend Steven Carew tiptoed into the room and took his daughter's hand gently. 'We have been so worried. What a blessing it is to see you sitting up and looking better.'

You came a long way, Pa, Vita wrote on her pad.

'Yes, indeed, and such weather! But Miss Navarro is a marvellous hostess, though I must say she is very unconventional in many ways. Her habit of dressing like a cowhand, for one thing. But she has been most kind to us. She and your aunt are firm friends now. Louisa is painting a very fine portrait. But we have all had sleepless nights, my dear. There were moments when we thought we had lost you.'

Many dreams. Very strange, Vita wrote.

'Your fever was strong.' He patted her hand. 'You did seem to be in another world at times. It is only to be expected.'

Vita turned the page back on her pad and showed her father the note she had written for her brother. *I failed Physics!* adding, *I'm sorry, Papa*.

'You must not trouble yourself. All your energies must be directed towards recovering your health. Your studies are not important for the time being.'

The door opened and Louisa came in, accompanied by a footman. He carried a large object swathed in a blanket. She directed him to place it at the foot of Vita's bed, where he propped it on a chair. Pulling aside the cover, Louisa revealed the strange portrait they had seen above the fireplace on their first evening. The portrait of the previous owner.

Vita's father and aunt both looked searchingly at the painting.

'Why have you brought it here, Louisa?' Reverend Carew asked. 'It is a peculiar thing. Perhaps this is considered a modern style of painting. It is not one I can admire, I must say.'

'It is unusual in its style, certainly,' Louisa said. 'But not without interest. I have brought it here to offer Vita an occupation. One that will encourage her to remain in bed and silent, whilst at the same time piquing her curiosity.'

Louisa looked satisfied with herself as she said this.

'What is she to do? Make a copy of it?' asked Reverend Carew.

'Not at all. Perish that thought! No, I have been looking at it since we arrived, you see, and I have become convinced that this painting is some sort of puzzle.'

Vita and her father now peered even more closely at the canvas.

'What makes you say so?' Reverend Carew inquired. 'It looks simply like a rather grim and poorly executed portrait with an unpleasant pair of crows in the background.'

'That is exactly what a puzzle picture looks like.'

'I've never heard of a puzzle picture, Louisa. Are you sure you are not inventing this idea?'

'They were popular in the Middle Ages, Steven. I'm sure you've heard of the Bergerheim Triptych. It was said to have held the secrets of the great hidden treasure of the house of Anjou. The clothing and every detail of the background contained hidden clues. It took several centuries to work it all out. But when they were successful, the fortune was found.'

Reverend Carew, who had never heard of the Bergerheim Triptych but felt unwilling, even in his fifties, to show ignorance in front of Louisa, his younger sister, made no reply to this. He only peered even more closely at the painting, looking sceptical. 'So you are hoping to track down a great fortune by finding the secrets of this daub, are you? Well, I wish you good luck!'

A dinner gong was heard in the background.

'I shall be there in a moment. Steven, please go without waiting. I want a further word with Vita.'

The vicar patted his daughter's shoulder briefly and left.

'In all honesty, Dear, I have no idea whether any secrets are hidden in this portrait, but I thought it might be of some interest. There is a label on the back.'

She turned the canvas to show a paper label glued to the back of the canvas. They both read Joseph Belmont. Garston Lacey.

'I doubt a lost fortune is hidden in this picture, but there is a great deal about the castle and its owners that Consuela Navarro does not know. She has been telling me about its history. She herself is really only interested in her horses. As far as she is concerned, the castle is only a convenient annex to a very good set of stables. But she is mildly curious and would be happy for you to ask a few questions. This portrait is something that has annoyed her for some time, so she is glad to be rid of it. And if you would like to study it for a while, so much the better, she says. Now I must go for dinner. It will be beef. Argentinians eat a great deal of beef. It is delicious, but unvarying. If only Monsieur were here. He is in France, you know. Visiting his mother.'

Vita looked at her aunt, amazed.

'Yes, I was taken aback myself. Monsieur has never confided his age to me, but I'd say he's in his seventies. His mother is in her nineties. It is not unusual to live to such an age in her village in Normandy, according to Monsieur. He puts it down to the cider. I hope he brings some back with him. It is marvellous to see you looking better, Dear. Maria is coming with your soup. I'll call in later.'

CHAPTER 10

*O*nce alone, Vita, taking her notebook out, began to write. The main features of the portrait were the young woman in grey and the birds. As she studied it, Vita became uncomfortably aware that the subject of the portrait was familiar to her. The face was the younger face of the night nurse who had visited in her fever. Was she real, this enigmatic night nurse? It was embarrassing to ask people about figures from a dream. She had said a lot of strange things. She had appeared vague and ethereal, she drifted in and out, but not ghostly in any sense that Vita understood.

She lay back on her pillows, thinking. The examiners in long black gowns, they were certainly a dream. But there were other visitors it was more difficult to be sure about. The child who came and went a few times, for example. Which category did he fall into?

How unstraightforward it seemed, all of a sudden.

She dozed for a while, and was woken by Maria with soup. Maria covered the portrait with its blanket as soon as she came into the room. Either she did not care for it, or she did not think Vita should have to face it while she drank her soup.

'I don't like these bad birds always looking at me,' she remarked, with a nod towards the covered painting.

Taking soup was still an effort, so Vita did not ask what Maria meant. She longed to ask about the inconvenient discovery in the icehouse, but had no strength for it that night.

On his visit the next day, Dr Haslam was able to examine the throat without causing agony or needing several people to hold Vita down. He declared himself content with the healing of the scar.

May I speak? Vita wrote on her pad.

'Not yet. We don't want to risk another flare-up,' he said. 'There could be permanent damage to the vocal cords if another infection were to set in.'

When nobody was in the room, she had made a few attempts at speaking. The voice seemed to work, but she did not want to risk it any further.

Did you see the body they found? she wrote.

'Yes. I know you have an interest in such matters.'

Dr Haslam seemed reluctant to say more. He sighed. 'I really am too preoccupied with my own work attending to the living to get embroiled in all this. Some unfortunate who died a very long time ago. A workman, I imagine. The police are sending someone. A coroner's officer. I believe he is expected tomorrow. '

Have the remains been moved?

'To a cold store room here in the castle.' Haslam was offhand. The matter was clearly of no interest to him. 'I imagine the coroner will want to take them away for further examination when he comes.'

May I get out of bed? I feel strong enough.

Haslam shook his head. 'I would recommend at least another day or two of bed rest,' he said. 'You have been dangerously ill, Miss Carew. It may not be in your nature to do so, but you must rest. I have left instructions with Miss Navarro that nobody is to bother you, or involve you in any way with the unfortunate find made in the garden. It is hardly urgent. The remains have clearly been there for many years. My recommendation is that you keep well away. Leave all that to someone else.'

IT WAS dark and windy outside that night. After Vita had received goodnight visits from her brother, father and aunt, and taken a little more soup from Maria, she sat in bed listening to the rain pounding the windows. She could see lights moving in the garden and went to the window to look out, but could make out nothing except a string of lanterns in the distance, swaying and bobbing in the wind far across the park. She wondered what they could be marking, and whether they had been there before, but had no recollection. It could be that the icehouse was kept lit now at night, though what reasons there might be for doing so, she had no idea.

Pleased to find that she could walk without feeling giddy, she decided to venture as far as the small library in the entrance lobby nearby. Surely there could be no harm in a little reading? She wrapped a shawl around her shoulders and stepped outside her room for the first time since she had arrived.

The library lobby was chilly. The bookshelves were mainly packed with large leather-bound volumes, which looked as if nobody had touched them for years, and which were almost all in Latin. Over on one side, there was a set of the plays and poems of Shakespeare, and a few volumes, but only a few, of an old Encyclopaedia Brittanica. That, at least, might offer a little varied reading, she thought. She reached for one of the volumes, but as she did, she heard footsteps pass the hall door.

There was nothing particularly strange about this, she told herself. Guests and staff must pass regularly.

But looking down, she could see there was no light shining under the door from outside. She opened the door slowly and peered along the arched stonework of the castle passage. It was so dark that she could see no further in either direction than the area lit by the soft light cast from behind her in the bedroom. The passage faded into utter darkness after about six feet, but in the distance there was still the echo of footsteps. The passer-by must be walking in the dark.

Vita stepped back into the book-lined lobby and closed the door. She pulled the large volume of the encyclopaedia off the shelf–it was heavier than she had expected–and was about to carry it back to the bedroom when the footsteps out in the corridor returned. They approached, then paused. Whoever it was would be able to see the light coming from her side of the door.

It was most likely, Vita thought, to be someone calling in to make sure the patient was still recovering. The old night nurse or Maria. Why, then, did they not enter?

The footsteps moved again, closer to the other side of the door. Someone appeared to be listening outside. Vita's instinct was to hold her breath and clutch the large volume she was holding to her chest.

From the other side of the great oak door, Vita heard a prolonged sigh–almost a groan. The sound of someone close to despair. A man. There was a scuffing sound, as if he were moving around, pacing this way and that. Then another groan and the foot-steps slowly receded.

It was an instinctive reaction to follow. Vita did not believe in ghosts or visitations–this was a flesh and blood visitor–and she needed to prove that to herself, and to know what he was about. There must be an explanation. She pushed the book she was holding back onto the shelf and hurried after the figure, but the passageway grew dimmer as she left behind the light of her room.

The chill in the corridor was the first thing that surprised her. The sickroom had been heated through-out–a fire night and day–but here the stonework seemed to release a damp cold into the air.

In modernised parts of the castle, Miss Navarro had installed generous electric lighting, but here there was no sign of a switch. It was a mistake, Vita soon realised, to have come without a candle, but she could hear the footsteps in the distance, so she pressed on, one hand on the cold stone of the wall to guide her.

After passing half a dozen doors, the corridor led to a vast, high-ceilinged gallery. The only light here was from the embers of a fire still burning in a great fireplace at one end. By this, Vita could make out a dark figure. He was thirty feet away, but Vita recog-nised the dark-suited figure of the butler, Wagstaff.

She pressed her back to the wall and watched as he stood looking into the fading fire, then paced a little up and down in front of it making an odd gesture with both his hands fisted, as if trying to screw up his courage and urge himself into action. In the shadowy light of the fireplace, his face was pale, the eyes, by contrast, dark and sunken. He was muttering to himself, but his words were lost in the distance.

As her eyes adjusted, Vita could make out rows of hunting trophies studding the wood panelling on every side. Stags, mostly, their mighty antlers reaching into the darkness high above, but also boar, and here and there more exotic game: several antelope and gazelle, a pair of tigers, and in pride of place over the fireplace, the mounted head of a huge elephant, his trunk raised, his curving tusks flickering in the light of the embers. The Mountfitchets were huntsmen who travelled widely and clearly spared no expense in transporting their trophies home.

There were few things Vita found less appealing than the heads of dead animals mounted on a wall, but among the creatures in the long gallery, there was one collection she found particularly repellent: the crows.

Where the larger animals lowered down from around the gallery at a height of about ten feet, the taxidermy crows were at eye level. Some stood on pillars or in glass cases, others perched on stone ledges or branches fixed to the woodwork. They were posed in every kind of position. Some seemed to eye the onlooker with malevolent calculation. Others had their beaks open in a silent shriek, or their wings raised as if about to attack. The Mountfitchet coat of arms, built into the fireplace in engraved stone, featured a glaring crow. Successive earls were extremely proud of their emblem, Vita concluded, with a shudder.

A clock nearby startled her by whirring suddenly before striking loudly three times, the chimes echoing harshly round the gallery. Vita gasped, her heart pounding. Wagstaff started too and seemed to look her way. There was a moment where Vita thought she might escape by shrinking back into the dark door-way, but it was too late. He had seen her and hurried over.

'Miss Carew! Are you unwell? Shall I call someone?'

Vita held her shawl more tightly around her, suddenly aware of the chill. 'I am not unwell, but I couldn't sleep. I heard noises.'

'The castle is ancient. Its timbers are prone to creaking in damp weather. Is there anything I can bring you?'

'No. I should be grateful, though, if you could show me the way back to my room. I have lost my bearings.'

'Of course. If you would care to follow me.'

The butler seemed his normal self, instead of the fretful man she had seen before. He led her back along the stone passages.

'Are there no lights?' Vita asked. 'It all seems very dark.'

'No electric lights in this part of the castle yet, Miss,' he said.

'And yet you move so surely and carry no lantern.'

He gave a slight laugh. 'Oh, I am used to it.'

'You are on duty at a very late hour.'

'It is my habit, Miss. I sleep very little. I like to keep an eye on the place at night.'

'You never find it… daunting? Going about this ancient place alone in the dark?'

'Not I. I have known it since a child.'

'It is reputed to be haunted, as I'm sure you know.'

'That sort of thing does not bother me, Miss,' he said. They had reached her bedroom door. He held it open.

He wished her good night and closed the door behind her.

Well, if you are not troubled by ghosts, you are certainly troubled by something else, Vita thought.

Only as she stepped over the threshold did she realise that she had been speaking normally to the butler instead of staying mute, as the doctor ordered.

CHAPTER 11

*E*dward was dressed strangely when he visited in the morning. He wore loose trousers, a white shirt and an embroidered sash and a strange red hat like an overgrown beret. 'I am a gaucho!' He declared, parading before his sister. 'Miss Navarro's men have recruited me to their brotherhood on the strength of my ability to throw a ring over a stick. It was pure luck, but they are a friendly crowd.'

Vita had no idea what he was talking about. She wrote a large question mark on her notepad.

Edward threw himself into a chair. 'Argentina sounds a fine country. I may visit. Miss Navarro's men are herdsmen and horse trainers. She brought half a dozen of them with her. Fine men. They speak a little English, luckily. I was at a loose end yesterday, so I went to admire the horses. Marvellous animals, pretty as a picture and very lively and clever. Anyway, I went to see them in the stables and the men invited me to ride, and we ended up racing and playing this game with rings.'

He sprang from the chair and executed a little dance, holding his hands above his head and stepping from side to side. 'It was the feast of Saint Some-thing-or-Other yesterday, they said, so they were having a party. I was invited. And now I am an honorary gaucho. The hat is particularly fine, don't you think?'

It was fine, she thought, marvelling at her brother's ability to find fun in any situation.

Edward stopped dancing and went stealthily to the door, opening it and checking outside before he continued. 'Have you had any dealings with the butler, Sis? I swear he keeps hanging about. I imagine it perhaps. But he seems always to be near your room. Over-attentive, perhaps. Are you still on the mend, by the way?'

Yes. But I am not permitted to speak or get up. Vita wrote, making a face.

'Pa will come and see you soon. He's been writing letters. He's busy with his next book on moths. Did he tell you? He has a new illustrator, a widow lady called Mrs Oliver. Do you remember her?'

Vita shook her head.

'She's very talented, he says. Just between us, I

think our Papa might be a little sweet on Mrs Oliver. Would you mind that? I mean, the old parent taking up with a lady?'

Vita wasn't sure. *It would depend on the lady*, she wrote.

Edward nodded and turned his attention to the portrait at the foot of the bed. 'So, have you found the secrets of the weird portrait yet? Where shall we dig for the buried treasure?'

Vita could only shrug.

'The crows must mean something, I suppose,' Edward said. 'And this is Lady Caroline, the mad Countess.' Edward bent and looked closely at the painting for a couple of minutes, then stood up and stretched his back. 'I find most puzzles dreary. I should hate, in particular, to spend very long with this painting. There's something distinctly eerie about it. I'm due to ride with the gauchos again soon. They play a sort of polo, you know. Like polo, but faster and, as far as I can see, without rules of any sort. Enormous fun. I'll leave you to the mysteries of this gloomy lady. Don't let her give you the heebie-jeebies. See you later.'

WONDERING HOW TO START, Vita looked the painting over again. It was a sombre, full length portrait. The subject stood with one hand to her small waist, the delicate fingers elegantly splayed. The other hand rested lightly on a polished wooden table. Also on the table there stood a strange example of taxidermy. Beneath a shining glass dome, a large stuffed crow stared in glass-eyed menace out at the viewer. One of its claws clasped the limp body of a small, brightly plumed bird, its head dangling–a dead kingfisher whose bright blue feathers were the brightest spot by far in what was otherwise a muted, almost mono-chrome image. On the wall behind the sitter's left shoulder hung a birdcage with a live black crow, much smaller than the stuffed one, inside. The second crow, too glared piercingly out at the onlooker.

The lady herself looked out with large, pale eyes. Her expression was difficult to interpret. It was unsmiling; the mouth was tight-lipped, the jaw and chin firmly set. The eyes held, perhaps, a suggestion of challenge. Her hair was dark, fastened high up behind her head, but softly curling at her temples and forehead. She would undoubtedly, Vita thought, be considered a beauty, but the extreme pallor of her face and hands, accentuated by the shadowy wall behind, was startling. It was a corpse-like milk-white with the smallest hints of grey and blue.

Vita was disturbed by a polite knock, followed by the appearance in the room of an anxious-looking Wagstaff.

'Excuse me, Miss Carew. I have no wish to disturb… Ah! I see you are looking at the portrait.'

Vita nodded. Wagstaff came a little closer to the bedside and stood to attention.

He was small, she thought, as butlers go. Usually the kind of households that ran to butlers favoured the taller man, as being more imposing and authoritative. Wagstaff was neat and smart in his suit, but probably no more than five feet three inches tall. His grey hair was trimmed tight to the sides of his head. It was difficult to guess his age.

She wrote, *I am not permitted to speak. I can only write notes,* and showed him the notepad.

He nodded. 'I am aware. I will not take much of your time. I am glad to see you are recovering. I wanted only to...' he faltered at this point '... to ask your help. It is irregular, I know.'

She looked at him questioningly.

'I have been here for many years,' he said, faltering under her gaze.

You knew the Countess? Vita wrote, indicating the portrait.

'I did.'

'I'm interested to know more about her,' Vita wrote on her pad.

He said no more, but looked at the portrait. Vita thought he looked unhappy. She could only wait.

'I was a lad, working in the kitchens when she was here as a bride. I only saw and heard what any servant would, but we all knew she was unhappy. The old Earl was well known for behaving cruelly towards her. He treated everyone badly. It was no surprise.'

An unhappy household, Vita wrote on her pad, wondering why the butler was telling her all this.

He nodded. 'He made her doubt her own mind. Told her things that frightened her. He paid people from the village–some would do anything he asked for a few pounds, or a bit off their rent. There was a family called the Pinkneys. Their lads used to run about at night, howl in the hall, make scratchings and banging noises. To scare her. She was never strong in her mind. It was easy to frighten Lady Caroline.'

Had she no family to turn to? Vita wrote.

'Only her father, but he had arranged her marriage with Mountfitchet. He was elderly and would not act against the Earl.'

They both looked at the portrait again.

Vita wrote, *What was she like?*

'I was only a boy, but from what I could tell, she was shy and gentle. Defenceless. She was kind to the staff. Even after she was taken away, she would write good wishes if she heard that someone was ill, and she never forgot to send each of us a little Christmas money.'

Wagstaff looked down at the polished toes of his shoes and shook his head. 'This is all thirty years ago, or more. The Earl wanted Lady Caroline declared mad. Doctors came from London to ask her questions. Lawyers too. To decide. If she was mad, he could take over her whole fortune. Have her declared unfit. That was what the Earl wanted.'

Vita waited, looking at the painting, then wrote, *he was successful*?

The butler nodded his head. 'He had her locked up in an asylum. Willowtree House in Garston Lacey.'

Her property and fortune?

'He took control of it. But soon after that, he went missing. Nobody heard of him again.'

She looked questioningly at the butler, before writing, *He just left?*

'They believed at first that he was in France. He had property in France. Or that he was travelling in Ireland. There were searches–the police and so on. It went on for years.'

You were a boy at this time? Vita wrote.

He nodded. 'Ten or eleven years old. I was the kitchen boy. I saw things that made no sense to me then, but they might make sense now.'

Vita said nothing, but looked at him steadily.

He shrugged and looked away again. 'I heard your aunt talking to Miss Navarro. You have a talent for solving mysteries, she said. I have questions that have been with me for so long. I have tried, over the years, but on my own I cannot work the answers out. I thought perhaps you might be able to assist me. I know how ill you have been, Miss Carew. I do wrong to ask, perhaps, but I have nowhere to turn.'

To Vita's alarm, the butler let out a ragged sigh. His face lost its professional composure. He seemed close to tears.

What can I do? she wrote.

Wagstaff fidgeted, as if struggling with a decision. 'You study medicine, I believe,' he said. 'I heard them say you work also with the Police Surgeon. You are educated. People will answer questions if you ask them. Questions even about the remains they found in the old ice house.'

Vita nodded, but wrote, *I am confined to this room. I should not even speak.*

Wagstaff sank suddenly into the chair beside the bed. A butler, sitting in the presence of a guest! It was another startling detail Vita later found difficult to believe.

He leaned towards her, speaking low and urgently. 'I saw something, you see, as a child. I saw the body of a young woman. She was lying at the bottom of the great stairs first thing in the morning. Her neck was broken, I think. It has haunted me ever since.'

Had she fallen? Vita wrote.

'I did not see what happened. I've always thought she fell over the banister. It is high. The floor is stone. It would be enough to kill,' Wagstaff said.

Who was she?

'I have no name. She was one of many guests. The house was either empty when the Earl was in

London or it was full to the rafters with crowds of guests when he was here.'

Did nobody else see her? Vita wrote.

He pointed to the portrait of the pale countess. 'The Earl did. He hid her body in a cupboard. I've never been sure, but I believe the countess saw her too.'

The death was never spoken of? Vita wrote.

'Not to me. And not to anyone else, from what I heard,' Wagstaff said. He sat back suddenly in the chair and ran his hand over his face. 'It was as if that poor dead lady had never been there. You are the first person I have ever told.'

They both looked at the pale lady in the portrait. Vita struggling to take in what the butler had said.

He hid the body?

'I saw him put it in a hidden cupboard under the stairs.'

And after that?

'It was gone when I looked later.'

And you saw nothing else unusual?

'Nothing,' Wagstaff said. 'But I worked in the yard and the kitchen, Miss. I rarely left it, and never came upstairs.'

Vita looked again at the dark lady with the intense eyes in the painting.

You think the remains that were found in the grounds could be the lady you saw dead? she wrote, holding the note out to him.

Wagstaff read it and shrugged. 'I don't know. She can't just have disappeared. I have spent my life trying to work out what happened to her. No trace has ever been found.'

Vita wrote, *Was there no search for her? No enquiry at the time?*

'Not that I know of, but as I said, I was just a child.'

They both paused. It was raining outside again. Vita wrote. *I am confined here. I can do so little. I'm not sure I can help in any useful way.*

Wagstaff read the note, and his expression brightened. It touched Vita to see how much even a suggestion of willingness relieved him.

'Just by thinking about it, you might see something I have missed,' he said. 'And people will answer your questions. But you must not be over-exerted. I understand that, of course.'

He stood, straightened the cuffs of his jacket and began to back away. Stopping suddenly, he added, 'I have her shoe, by the way.'

Vita looked confused.

'The fallen lady's shoe. It came off, and I picked it up. I have kept it hidden all these years. Should I bring it for you to see?'

Vita could only nod.

He left, saying, 'I am grateful to you, Miss Carew,' as the door closed behind him.

CHAPTER 12

hen her aunt came in later, she sat on Vita's bed and they looked the portrait over together. They were drinking tea. Vita's throat was recovered to the point where this was only slightly uncomfortable.

'I have spent some time wondering what makes this picture so strange,' her aunt said. 'There are the obvious things, such as that vicious-looking crow with a poor dead victim in its claw, but there are details too. I wondered for several days why the lady's gaze is so haunting, but if you look very closely at her eyes…'

They both peered intently.

'You will see there is a dab of that kingfisher blue in the pupil. It's almost invisible, but it has the effect of unsettling her gaze. Do you see? All that one notices from a distance is that her eyes are subtly odd. And if you look again, you can see that same tiny hint of blue in the eyes of the caged bird, too.'

Vita wrote on her pad, *crow on the Earl's coat of arms?*

'Oh, yes,' her aunt said, 'nasty-looking crows everywhere on shields and crests around the castle.'

He had a signet ring with one, Vita wrote.

'I expect so,' said her aunt. 'He was apparently very proud of the crow emblem. A dreadful man, by all accounts. Miss Navarro said nobody would speak of him when she first came. Two or three of the old staff were still here, but they would not be drawn about the Earl.'

Wagstaff spoke to me a little about the past, Vita wrote.

'How strange,' said Louisa. 'I wonder Consuela kept Wagstaff on at all. He is no great shakes as a butler–willing enough, but not very skilful, and rather too omnipresent for my liking. One wants an attentive butler, but constantly lurking is not the right idea at all. He seems never to leave my peripheral vision, and when he does, one imagines him listening at the keyhole. Ten to one, he is outside the door now.'

He asked me to help him, Vita wrote. *He seems worried about matters from the past.*

'I hope you sent him packing. You are not to bother yourself with Wagstaff. You have been seriously ill, Vita. You must devote your energies to recovering. Never mind the worries of a strange butler.' She looked irritably around the room. 'This must have been a dreadful place when the Earl was here. He is reputed to have driven his young wife mad and sent her into an insane asylum.'

So that he could take control of her fortune? Vita wrote.

'Yes. Well, that is Consuela's belief. There were a number of similar scandalous cases in my youth. Something to do with the Married Women's Property Act,' said her aunt, sipping her tea. 'Before it, a husband became the master of all his wife's assets upon marriage. After it, a wife retained some control. That did not suit men like the Earl of Mountfitchet. There was no money on his side of the family, so he wanted his wife's, and the way to get it was to have her declared incapable due to insanity. He wasn't the only man to try it. In his case, the plan seems to have worked very well. She was always frail, mentally, they say. He drove her to madness, had her put in a lunatic asylum, and spent a great deal of her fortune before he disappeared.'

They both looked back at the painting.

When did the Countess die? Vita wrote.

'I couldn't say. She can't be more than twenty-five in this portrait.' Louisa stood quite suddenly and put her teacup on the nightstand. 'Vita, your father wants a word with you about Mrs Oliver.'

Edward mentioned her name, Vita wrote, waiting to see what her aunt would add.

'She is a great talent as a botanical artist, apparently. And lately she has collaborated with Steven on his book about moths.' Her aunt's face had an odd, set expression, Vita thought.

Have you met her? Vita's writing took on a sudden slant. Her aunt noticed.

'Once or twice at the vicarage. A nice enough woman, but not particularly interesting. A Devonshire country lady, but with airs, if you know what I mean. She has a daughter about your age; Evelyn, a little pudding of a thing when we met, but that was some years ago. Anyway, I thought I'd just mention Mrs Oliver so that it didn't come as too much of a shock. He hasn't said anything officially, yet.'

She will be a help to him in the parish, I imagine, Vita wrote. Her aunt raised her reading glasses to read the note, but then flung them loose again on their chain, rather impatiently.

'She will paint moths beautifully, no doubt, but tramping miles in the rain to deliver food to the old and sick as you did for years, is not Mrs Oliver's style at all. She is far too conscious of her station in life. She is distantly related to the Bishop of Exeter, and mentions it at every opportunity. Her daughter is about to marry a captain in the Royal Navy. Which makes her practically royalty in Devon, as you know.'

You do not care for the Olivers? Vita wrote with a look of innocence.

'If my brother seeks a companion, it is not for me to question his choice,' Louisa said crisply. 'But I must say, I have always considered exact illustrations of nature to be the dullest artistic endeavour on earth. I know it is an unpopular view. Most people love a pretty moth on a bramble, complete with thorns and one shiny blackberry. Marvellous! So true to life! they cry, how admirable! I can't abide them. But I, as you know, am considered a dangerous revolutionary when it comes to art.'

Louisa took a deep breath and patted her niece's arm. 'Ignore me, Vita. My opinion is of no consequence. It is you and Edward who will gain a moth-painting step-mother. And your Papa will at least have a helpmate. Of sorts. I am afraid, though, that Mrs Oliver will exert a powerful influence over my brother. She has already altered his views substantially on one or two significant matters, if my conversations with him are anything to go by.'

Louisa smoothed her niece's pillow and put her hand briefly to Vita's forehead. 'But you must not worry yourself about anything like that now. You must rest and continue to regain your strength. It has been a difficult few days for us all, but for you above all. I can hardly tell you how delighted I am to see you on the mend. There were moments when we thought we could lose you, Dear.'

Vita was moved to see a tear swiftly brushed away as Louisa stood to leave.

When she was alone, she looked out into the dim room and regretted putting her family through such anxiety there in the strange surroundings of Crowswood.

CHAPTER 13

*A*fter her aunt had left, Vita looked over her notes on the portrait. She added *kingfisher?* And *kingfisher blue?* and looked again at Lady Caroline's eyes, with their unsettling dot of that colour, and how it reflected the dead kingfisher in the clutch of the crow and linked them to the smaller caged crow on the other side.

Large Crow = Mountfitchet? she wrote. That part was relatively straightforward. Small caged crow–ah, it became clearer after what her aunt had said, *small crow = Lady Caroline?*

And the small crow was caged, just as Lady Caroline had been locked in the asylum. So why was the caged crow looking so intently at the large one that the bright pearly blue of the kingfisher's plumage was reflected in its eyes? And why, since she was not looking at the kingfisher, but out at the viewer, did the same blue appear in Lady Caroline's sad eyes?

She saw something? Vita wrote. *Something blue.*

IT WAS LATE when Wagstaff returned with the shoe. Once he had reassured himself that Vita was still awake, he placed a tissue wrapped object on the bed, and watched as she unwrapped its many layers.

The little satin slipper was perfectly preserved. It was embroidered with gold thread, had an elegant heel and a white silk lining. Its overall colour was a bright, almost luminous kingfisher blue.

Beautiful! Vita wrote.

Wagstaff nodded. 'I have looked after it for all these years. As a kitchen lad with no room of my own, it was not easy to keep it safe. It was such a pretty, finely made thing. I didn't own pretty things. I didn't own anything. I knew there'd be terrible trouble if anyone found me with it.'

They both smiled at the shoe, which seemed to shimmer where it caught the firelight.

Vita examined it. It was finely made. Expensive, she guessed. No maker's name appeared inside, which seemed unusual. It must have been made to order, but not by the usual sort of shoemaker, because a commercial company would include a name or label of some sort, surely? The sole, which was white leather, had no embossed name either, and it was barely marked, as if the shoe had hardly been worn, and had certainly never stepped out of doors.

Turning it over in her hand, Vita pictured the wearer as a small woman. It was certainly two sizes smaller than her own shoe size. She glanced at Wagstaff and saw the fondness with which he watched the shoe being admired.

'It was all I had, you see. Nobody ever spoke of her. Nothing was ever said. It was only this shoe that proved I really had seen her. Without it, I could've believed I'd imagined or dreamed there was a poor dead lady's body there that morning. Kept me sane, that little shoe did, all these years. Thirty-one years. I counted them on the way here. And the funny thing is, I have hardly even looked at it in all that time. I tucked it away. Just knowing it was there was enough.'

He is only in his early forties, Vita thought, doing the calculation. *He looks a lot older. Life has not been kind to Wagstaff.*

As he spoke, Vita continued to examine the shoe. It was shaped for a left foot. The upper was lined with white satin, the sole with soft white suede. As she ran her hand inside the shoe, she felt a set of small ridges at one side. Peering closely, she could make out a row of tiny embroidered letters. She held the shoe up to the firelight, but the room was dim. She pointed to a lamp, but Wagstaff shook his head. It was tethered by its electric cable.

He lit a candle instead and held it closer. It was still difficult to make anything out.

I need my spectacles, Vita wrote.

It took the butler several minutes to locate the spectacles on a dresser at the other end of the room. Vita had not worn them for many days. Everything slid into clear focus as she put them on, and holding the shoe to the candlelight, she could at last make out four miniscule letters embroidered in the palest pink silk into the white lining: MIMI.

MIMI. She wrote it on her pad for Wagstaff.

'Her name?' he asked. 'Her name was Mimi?'

Vita could only shrug her shoulders. *Or the sign of the shoemaker? Or a maker's reference or code?*

Wagstaff held up the shoe and turned it in the light, squinting to see the letters for himself.

Was there a guest by that name? Have you heard it before? Vita wrote.

'Never,' he said, but then repeated the name several times, smiling. 'Thank you, Miss Carew.'

'Did anything else happen that day? What do you remember?' she wrote.

Wagstaff looked again at the shoe. 'I was on my way to the servants' rooms upstairs. I had two jugs of hot water. It was my job first thing to carry it up to them. They were heavy. I was told to take them one at a time, but I liked to carry both at once, to save time. I was taking the short way, which I shouldn't have, across the main hall, because it was quicker, but I caught my foot on something. I fell. The water went everywhere. It was a lady lying there, dead. The Earl came. I didn't see where from. He pulled my ear and sent me away. At first I ran to the kitchen, but then I went back. I hid in a corner and watched him pick the lady up, and hide her in a cupboard that's hidden in the panelling under the stairs. He went and fetched the keys, came back and locked it.'

And the shoe? Vita wrote.

'When he first sent me packing–gave me a good kick–I saw it in a corner, under one of the tables. I grabbed it without thinking.'

And later?

'After he locked the door, Mr Warren, the old butler, came down. The master told Warren to delay breakfast and to send for his horse. Said he wanted to ride out early.'

Did he often go out early?

'Never. He was a late riser.'

How long was he gone for? Vita wrote.

'He was back in less than an hour. I saw him ride in.'

Where could he reach on horseback in that time?

Wagstaff shrugged. 'The village? The main Norwich road?'

What's there?

96

'In the village? A few cottages, a church, a general store, a public house.'

You mentioned a family called the Pinkneys before. Where did they live?

'At the edge of the village.'

And they did things for the Earl. Boys ran about at night, and so on?

'They did. They were well known as a crooked lot. Poachers, thieves. Always out to make a few shillings.'

Vita nodded. She turned a page in her notebook and wrote, *The old butler. What was he like?*

'Mr Warren? He was the proper, old-fashioned sort of butler. He'd served the Earl's father, the third Earl, and was very devoted to the old man, but he never took to the son. It broke his heart to see the castle full of scandal and bad behaviour, but he'd never have said so. Stiff and formal, he was. Kept himself a bit apart from the rest of the servants. But he was fair. The staff liked old Warren.'

Did you like him?

Wagstaff ran a finger over the shoe he still held in his hand. 'Like him? I couldn't say. He was one of the great powers of the castle, and I was just a kitchen lad. I did not fear him, at least. He did not beat me for no reason. Many others did.'

He wrapped the shoe in its paper again, and carried it away, saying he did not want to tire her further.

Vita leaned back on her pillows. She pictured the shoe and its unmistakable colour. That blue. The same blue, surely, that was reflected in the eyes of the caged crow and the Countess in the portrait. So the blue in her eyes was telling viewers of the portrait that Lady Caroline saw the killing. Someone called Mimi was the victim, and Mountfitchet, represented by the crow with the dead kingfisher clasped in his cruel claw, must be the killer.

But what to do about an unreported murder more than thirty years in the past and hinted at in a strange picture? Tell the police?

Of course, if the remains found in the ice house turned out to be the body of this mysterious Mimi, the matter would at least partially be solved. The victim would be identified. But hadn't Wagstaff said the coroner's officer was going to take them away tomorrow?

Vita removed her spectacles and tried to sleep. A gusty wind was rattling the windows. Somewhere in the distance, a loose shutter tapped repeatedly. Timbers creaked. Mice scuttled in the wood panelling behind the bed head. A barn owl shrieked nearby.

I must see the remains for myself.

She could, she thought, wait until the next day and then calmly persuade her aunt and father that she was perfectly well enough to perform an examination of a long-dead corpse.

It hardly seemed likely that they would agree.

Or she could take a look at it now, before anyone stopped her or took it away.

The answer seemed so obvious and definite that Vita climbed out of bed immediately and searched the room for her boots and coat. It was only when she was outside her bedroom door that she remembered she had only the haziest notion of the layout of the castle. Where had that great gallery been? The one where she had found Wagstaff among the hunting trophies and the silent crows? That seemed central and would make a good starting point. And besides, she told herself, the cold store, which had been mentioned as the resting place for the remains, must be in a basement. She obviously just needed to find a staircase and follow it down.

Equipped with her notebook and pencil and a candlestick, she slipped out of her room. Then returned to collect her spectacles and set off again.

CHAPTER 14

*S*he had expected the darkness of the castle's corridors, and the cold should also have been no surprise, but the gusts of icy wind that constantly threatened to blow out the candle were more than Vita had bargained for. A window or door must be open somewhere.

As soon as she stepped beyond the renovated wing, the temperature dropped even further and all light but the candle fell away. The stones felt damp and slippery to her hand on either side. The chill crept through the soles of her boots. It made her shiver. The smell in the air was of ancient mould, rust and damp.

Vita did not recognise the hallway. It was high and beamed with carved oak timbers. Heavy arched doors led off on either side. Had she passed this way the other night? There was no way to tell. Nothing looked familiar. The guttering candle smoked and a drop of scalding candle wax dripped onto her hand. It hurt enough to distract her. When she looked up, she thought she saw a hint of flickering movement ahead. Firelight? It might be the great gallery she had found Wagstaff in before. She hurried towards it.

The passageway narrowed suddenly and divided. Off on her right, a steep spiral staircase wound down into the darkness. To the left, the passage continued for only a few feet before—as far as she could tell by the flickering candlelight—ending in a solid wall. The trace of light she had seen ahead had now gone.

Vita took a deep breath. Perhaps setting out to find human remains at dead of night in a dark and reputedly much-haunted castle had not been the wisest choice. It would be sensible to go back to bed, she thought. Scientific thought, cool and objective, is needed to perform a post-mortem examination, and that is inhibited by the loud pounding of my own heart in my ears. It is not that I am afraid, exactly; it is just that rational thought is easily overpowered by... whatever is that smell? Was that a rat? I have seen that movement of something half-seen in the far distance several times now.

The spiral stairs were difficult. Vita's candle struggled to illuminate the tightly twisting treads. She raised the candlestick, and the candle hit a stone moulding she hadn't seen and fell at her feet, extinguishing itself. A black curtain of darkness dropped around her.

Usually, Vita had found in the past, when it seemed completely dark, a few moments were all it took for the eyes to adjust and begin to pick out shapes. Here on the stairs, there was no such adjustment. Vita stared into the darkness, and it remained dense, featureless, and utterly impenetrable.

But there was no staying there to freeze in the dank coil of these stone steps. She must move. Feeling about, she eventually found and reunited the candle and its brass stick. She had no matches to relight it. Shivering, and with one hand to the cold curving stones, she felt her way further down in the darkness, sliding her boots to feel the edge of each step. It took a lot of concentration.

She only noticed the shuffling behind her when it had been there for several minutes. A little sound, like a child feeling its way down the stairs further up. Vita held her breath to listen. It came again. The hair pricked on her neck. She could hear someone else breathing. They were coming closer. She tried to hurry, but only misplaced her foot on one of the steps and stumbled against the wall. It was then that she distantly heard voices from somewhere below. A trace of lamplight began to creep up the stairs. As she turned with relief towards it, the small shadowy figure of a child suddenly dashed past, pushing her aside, followed by a rush of cold air.

Vita cried out involuntarily. The voices below fell silent.

A few steps further down and light, flickering light from lanterns, slowly began to reach up to her.

'I shall return in an hour.' It was Consuela Navarro's voice. 'If she is no further on by then, she will need help. I told him he might be needed, but it is a fair distance, and the weather is bad.'

Vita hurried down the remaining turns of the spiral stairs and found Miss Navarro and Wagstaff standing inside a door. Wagstaff was still closing it behind them. Both had snow on their boots and the shoulders of their overcoats. They stamped and blew on their hands. Both looked astonished to see her emerge from the darkness.

'Are you unwell, Miss Carew? Do you need assistance?' Wagstaff asked, stepping forward.

Vita shook her head energetically to show she was well. She dug the notebook out of her pocket and wrote. *Thank you, I am quite well. I hoped to examine the remains before they are taken away.* Then added, *If you will permit it, Miss Navarro.*

'At this hour?' Consuela said. 'Why now, at night?'

Wagstaff answered the question. 'They are to be moved in the morning, Madam,' he said. 'The Coroner's officer is due to collect them.'

Consuela, preoccupied with something else, only nodded. 'I have no objection. Your aunt has said you have training in these matters. If you are interested, you can do as you wish. But not alone. You need assistance. Someone will be needed to hold a light.'

'I'll accompany Miss Carew, Madam, if you permit it.'

Consuela nodded. 'It is not a task I envy. You will find it cold down there. Do not stay too long,' she said, and walked away.

Wagstaff watched his mistress leave. He took off his great coat and hung it on a hook by the door. It seemed to be a door to a service yard, Vita thought. She wanted to ask why they were out there in the middle of the night, but it seemed an intrusive question, and besides, it would have been a slow one to write, so she just looked expectantly at Wagstaff.

'This way, Miss,' he said.

HAVING LOCATED and lit a lantern and Vita's candle, Wagstaff led the way along the service passage as far as a wide cobbled tunnel that led downwards.

'It is a horse tunnel, Miss,' he explained. 'They hid the horses and cavalrymen down here if the castle was attacked. There are underground stables and barrack rooms too.'

Vita followed him, imagining the noise of a crowd of horsemen clattering down the cobblestones, and how it must have smelt in these airless passages when they were in residence. It helped to distract her from wondering how she would deal with the remains she was due to examine. She had never seen a body that had been left for thirty-one years, or what remained of one. It had been in a cold place, but what that meant in terms of its preservation, she could only guess. She wished she had her laboratory coat with her. It offered only nominal protection, but was a regular companion in her work with the dead, and somehow it armed her for what she was about to see.

'It is in here,' Wagstaff said. He had stopped and was holding the lantern up to throw its light against a studded door. He opened it, and hung the lantern on a hook, illuminating a vaulted room with a wide stone shelf set into the wall on the far side. A pile of soil and rags lay on the shelf, looking as if someone had tipped them there thoughtlessly.

Vita put her hand into her pocket and found a scarf. She tied it round her head, grateful for the few moments this gave her to compose her thoughts. She wrote a question to Wagstaff on her notepad before beginning.

Did you help to carry the remains here?

He shook his head. He did not move towards the remains, but pressed himself into the door opening, reluctant to move closer. He had been calm and steady until now, but confronted with the pile of rags that represented a body, he seemed seized by something like dread.

'I cannot come closer, Miss.'

Vita gestured that she understood this and expected him to remain where he was. She carried her candle over and set it on the stone ledge, where it lit a series of strange marks and carvings on the curved stone walls. Ignoring them, Vita took a deep breath and approached the pile of damp earth and much begrimed clothing. She began to make notes as she carried out an initial inspection from left to right.

Presentation is of fabric, mildewed, apparently compressed and rotted. Colours indistinguishable. No obvious skeletal form on superficial inspection, except at the far right, where the top of a skull is partially discernible.

She lifted the candle stick and held it above the pale dome of the skull. This must have been what the workmen saw. As far as she could tell, it was intact, but the rest of the cranium, and the maxilla facial bones were buried in rotted material.

A decision now had to be made. Should she make notes, but leave the remains untouched, or should she continue with the examination? Vita knew that a police surgeon or coroner would want the remains preserved as closely as possible to the way they were found, but in this case, the disturbance had already taken place. What she was looking at was a heap of jumbled remains, thrown down by workmen horrified by what they had found and wanting to escape as quickly as possible.

She wrote in her notebook. *Did you see how the*

remains were brought here? But when she turned to show the question to Wagstaff, he was no longer at his post in the doorway. He could not bear to watch, she guessed, and went back to her task, having decided that as long as she documented what she found, there could be no objection to a closer examination of either clothing or remains, as long as she did not add or remove anything.

It was a painstaking task. The clothing encrusted, rigid, solidified, should ideally have been soaked off. Without water, she could only peel a little away. The remains were jumbled, so she found first a heel bone and the remains of the sole of a boot, and beneath it the edge of what appeared to be a detached thigh bone. In several sections, there were vertebrae and three or four ribs lay beneath a strip of lighter fabric. Poking with her pencil (the only equipment she had), Vita could find little else. The remains, as far as she could tell, amounted to little more than a skull, a partial spine, a few ribs and a single leg.

Having reached this conclusion and completed her notes, she lifted her candlestick and turned to leave. Wagstaff's pale face appeared in the doorway.

These remains are incomplete, Vita wrote. *It has been scraped up and cast down here with very little care.*

Wagstaff spoke, but he mumbled. Vita could not hear what he said. She turned to see him clutching the wall as if he might collapse. 'Is it the lady? The lady in blue?' he gasped at last.

Vita shook her head, unhooking the lantern and handing it back to the butler. She showed him her notepad. *This is a partial body. It is a man. A tall man.*

Wagstaff looked at her slowly, blinking. She saw the colour drain from his face, then his knees gave out and he sank slowly toward the cobblestone floor.

CHAPTER 15

*V*ita was kneeling beside the butler when the shout rang through the stone passage-ways of the castle above.

'Ai! La yegua, la pobre yegua!'

Wagstaff shuddered and came to himself. 'The mistress,' he said, 'her best mare is in foal.'

'La matara, la pobre! WAGSTAFF! Come quickly!'

Wagstaff struggled to his feet, straightened his tie, and flicked the dust from his suit. 'I said I would fetch the horse doctor.'

'Go. I'll follow you,' Vita told him.

Consuela was standing at the door to the service yard in a state of extreme anxiety. 'She is sick, Wagstaff. My men cannot help her. They are afraid. You must ride for the horse doctor. Be quick. Please

109

be quick. Tell him she is in danger. Please go. Go now!'

Wagstaff pulled his coat from its hook and rushed out.

'Can I help in any way?' Vita asked.

Consuela shook her head sadly. 'It is my prize brood mare, my Esperanza. She is in labour. She cannot birth the foal, you know? It will not move. She is in pain and exhausted. My men know horses, they know them well. They know births, even difficult ones, but they can do nothing to help her. We have watched her all night. I am afraid she will die. Do you know horses, Miss Carew? The horse doctor is half an hour away, at least.'

Vita did not know horses in any medical sense. She had spent an afternoon or two reading horse anatomy books at one time, but that was three years ago. She could only look uncertain.

Consuela, though, was desperate. 'Come,' she said. 'Take a look at her, at least. There may be something you can do. Please!'

Just as when they first met, Vita found it difficult to say no to Consuela. She soon found herself in the stables, where a glossy bay mare stood panting in the straw. Flecks of sweat lay on her flanks and when Vita put a hand to her neck, it felt clammy. It needed no expertise to tell that she was in pain.

'I must wash my hands,' Vita said. As she followed one of the gauchos to a sink and scrubbed her hands, she tried to picture the diagrams of horse anatomy she remembered from the library of Pemberton Hall. What she mainly recalled was that certain presentations of a foal in the birth canal were considered hopeless. All that could be done was to extract the poor foal in any way possible in the hope of saving the life of the mare. Vita could only pray this was not such a case.

As her next contraction took hold, the little mare groaned and raised her head, her back curving with the strain. Two small hooves, wrapped in white membrane, protruded already from her.

Vita knew this meant that the foal's head must be tucked back. Its nose should be visible between the hooves. A normal delivery was a neat head first dive into the world, but this little creature was looking backwards.

'Is my fault,' Consuela said. She was standing at the horse's head, stroking and speaking gently to her. 'The stallion was too large. His foal is too big for my poor Esperanza. Now I will kill her with this greed.'

'Your men deal with difficult births at home, surely?' Vita said. 'Can none of them resolve this by manipulation? I know it is often done.'

'In a simple case, yes, but with a foal in this position. They are afraid to try.'

'Do they know how it might be done? In theory, I mean.'

'In theory, they know, but they also know she is

my favourite. Each is afraid to do something that could kill her.'

Vita watched in pity as the contraction squeezed the little feet forward, but failed to make any progress, so they slipped back to the same place. Such neat little hooves.

Consuela looked sharply at Vita. 'If I tell them to instruct you, will you try? You know medicine. I am afraid to lose her before the horse doctor can get here.'

Vita looked once more at the mare, sighing and shifting from foot to foot with the pain.

'I may kill her myself, Miss Navarro.'

'I beg you to try, even so. Please.'

Vita nodded.

An older gaucho, a lean-faced man, was called. He stood against the wall and spoke in quiet Spanish to Consuela.

'He says you should put your hand into the birth canal and follow the legs to feel which way the neck is bent. The foal may by looking down between its front legs, or up and over its own back. Once the position is clear, he will tell you what to do next,' she said.

Vita rolled up her sleeve and began.

GROWING up in the Devonshire countryside had taught Vita much about animal life. She had witnessed a farmer help a cow deliver its calf, but she had never been involved in, or even witnessed, a difficult equine delivery.

Hours later, as she crept back into her bed, exhausted, she smiled to herself, thinking how varied the reactions to her studying science and medicine were. Many people assumed that as a young woman she knew nothing and was more or less useless; the rest assumed she knew everything and could perform instant miracles. Perhaps this was just a fact of medical life?

The mare, showing signs of exhaustion and distress, tolerated Vita's intervention with touching patience. Vita knew she must not be slow or tentative. She must mimic a confidence she did not feel, and she must move fast.

'Push your arm inside and tell me what you feel,' her instructor, who had been introduced as Roderigo, told her. He had already helped her roll her sleeve to the shoulder and rubbed white goose fat onto her arm.

She did as she was told and felt the foal's front legs, pushing her arm further to reach the curve of its shoulder. There it became more difficult. The fluid-filled birth sack still enclosed the foal, its tough and slippery membranes obscuring the outlines her hand sought to find.

'You must feel if the head is up or down,' Consuela translated.

Vita leaned in and was able with effort to move her hand further. She felt no throat or neck, only the contours of a shoulder. Pushing on, she thought she could discern the flex of the neck. 'Down. I think its head is down,' she said. Her voice, through lack of use, was little more than a croaky whisper.

This seemed to be good news to the gaucho adviser.

'We must bring the head up,' said Consuela. 'Usually, one would push the foal back to where there is more space, turn the little one to the side and bring the head forward that way. You may need to tie a rope to its lower jaw.'

Roderigo, standing closer now, held a rope.

'If there is no space,' Consuela added, 'and that may be the case here, we must simply haul the foal out by the front legs and risk the neck being damaged. This way does not usually end well, but we may save the mare's life, at least.'

The mare was hanging her head now, shivering her skin and groaning gently. Something was needed quickly.

Vita pushed her arm as far as she could reach. She was sure now that she could feel the foal's neck flexed downward. It was looking down between its two front hooves. As the contraction softened against

THE KILLING AT CROWSWOOD CASTLE

her arm, she applied pressure to the shoulder and was able to move it away.

'Take the leg furthest from you and pull it under to turn the shoulders,' Consuela said, translating Roderigo's words. 'Pull strongly.'

The leg was difficult to grasp. It felt slippery, but inside its membrane, also surprisingly sturdy. Spreading her fingers, Vita gripped and, holding her breath, pulled, gently at first, then more and more forcefully. She felt the foal respond with a brief shudder.

The mare shifted her back feet. Consuela stroked her neck and spoke gently to her, reassuring.

Vita caught her breath and tried again. Focusing all her efforts on the unseen hand, imagining it easing the shoulders round, rotating them to a place where the neck could unbend.

In the stables, all onlookers held their breath, too. The mare gave a drawn-out sigh. Vita gritted her teeth and pulled even more strongly than before. She felt a shift, an easing. The foal twitched and began to move for itself. Its shoulders rolled a little to the left. She could feel the neck tucked under now. But it still had to be straightened.

Vita's arm and shoulder were aching. Another contraction took hold. It squeezed the foal, but did not succeed in moving it any further into the world.

'You must reach in and tie this rope to the lower

jaw of the foal. It is harsh, but it is the only way to apply the pressure.' Consuela told her.

Vita looked at the rope and shook her head. She could not do it. Could not reach the jaw, let alone loop a rope through the poor creature's open mouth.

'I am afraid the mare is failing,' Consuela told her. 'She is swaying on her feet. If she goes down, it will make things worse. We will lose her too. You have done your best, Vita. Let us give her a rest. Roderigo will do what is needed to take the foal away. It is not likely to survive now, anyway.'

Roderigo nodded, grim-faced.

'No,' Vita said. 'I felt movement. One more try.'

She pressed the foal's shoulders away from her, pushing back into the birth canal as hard as she could. It felt brutal to shove so hard, but almost immediately, the foal responded. The combination of Vita's manipulation and pressure of the muscles squeezing around it, made the little animal squirm and jerk its head upward. Progress!

The mare, as this happened, swayed on her feet. Four other men sprang from the shadows in the stable and propped her upright. She must not go down now. She uttered a long, guttural groan.

Emboldened by the signs of life she felt in the baby, Vita slipped her hand around its shoulder and under its neck. *Come on! Come on! Just lift your head. That's it, a little more, more again. Keep going. Keep going.*

And then it was done. A damp nose emerged between the front hooves and with one more contraction, the slippery mess of spindly limbs and damp furry body that was a living foal fell out onto the straw.

The mare gave a soft sigh and fell to her knees and then on to her side. Nothing the gauchos could do would prevent it. They stepped forward and began immediately to work on the foal, brushing the membranes clear of its nose, using handfuls of straw to rub its flanks and stimulate its breathing.

But it needed no help. The gangly little thing raised its wobbly head immediately and snorted its first breath, twitching its ears.

Consuela and the men moved in, tending to mare and foal with practiced hands. Vita leaned against the stable wall, too tired to do more than smile weakly. Shortly afterwards two of the maids arrived and, one on either side, escorted her back to her room, helped her wash the goose grease from her arm, and put her into bed, making up the fire and drawing the curtains against a misty grey dawn.

CHAPTER 16

*W*hen he took her temperature on his visit the next day, Dr Haslam raised an eyebrow and looked sternly at his patient.

'I am afraid you may have been exerting yourself, Miss Carew. I am still recommending strict bed rest. Your constitution runs the risk of being permanently undermined by an infection such as the one you have just suffered. That is not a risk you should run.'

Vita wondered what, if anything, he knew about the previous night's activities. She wrote *May I speak?* On her notepad.

He shook his head. 'Not until your temperature is normal for three days in a row. It is for your own good. The vocal cords and tonsils must be given the chance to recover after the surgery.'

He returned the thermometer to its sterilising fluid and prepared to leave, but looked at Vita a little less sternly on his way to the door. 'Medical people make the worst patients. Doctors and nurses offer sensible advice, but in general they regard bed rest for themselves as torture. They complain when they are not completely fit again in half the expected time. It is absurd, but predictable. We make the very worst patients, Miss Carew. Now, I shall visit again the day after tomorrow. There is a visitor waiting. Shall I show him in?'

When Vita nodded, Haslam opened the door and spoke to the unseen person waiting outside. 'She is not permitted to speak. Make sure you keep the visit short, Gully. Miss Carew does not need to be worn out with your tall stories.'

The visitor was a jovial man in middle age with mud on his coat and boots. He carried a battered hat. His coat was of the kind that Vita usually saw on coachmen, with caped shoulders to keep the rain out. The bald top of his head was paler than his face, suggesting he wore the hat out in all weathers. His eyes were kind and his handshake very firm indeed. He introduced himself as Gulliver Colindale, the vet.

'Quite a night in the stables last night, Miss Carew, I hear!' He strode to the fire and warmed his hands at it.

Vita wasn't sure how the professional was going to react to whatever he had heard of her dealings with the mare and foal, so she only nodded warily in reply.

'I tried my best to get here, but the roads were

awash and we were stuck for half an hour in the ford at Haysmarsh. But I needn't have worried, eh? I must say, I was mightily impressed with your efforts. You saved them both, by all accounts. Miss Navarro is singing your praises. You are training as a medic, I hear.'

I hope to, Vita wrote.

'Well, you have a natural talent for it. It is not everyone who can assist in a difficult delivery of that sort. Can you tell me what you did?'

Vita wrote a brief description and showed it to Colindale.

'Ah,' he said, running his hand over his short brown beard as he read her scribbled notes, 'ventral retroflection. Difficult. Always difficult. But you saved the day. Or rather, you saved the foal! In any event, I have just seen a healthy young colt, none the worse for his difficult start in life, and a mare who is tired, but recovering well. If you weren't in your sick bed, I would set about persuading you to study veterinary medicine immediately!'

Not everyone is so enthusiastic about my studies, Vita wrote.

Colindale shrugged cheerfully, 'It's high time we used all the talent available, male or female, in my view. My daughter Emily has worked with me since she was ten years old. She is a fine veterinary assistant already and has her own plans to study. Of course, it isn't easy, but that won't stop the likes of

Emily or you, I'm sure, Miss Carew. Now, I must leave you to rest, or my esteemed colleague, Dr Haslam, will have my guts for garters.'

He strode towards the door, but then halted when struck by a thought. 'By the by, Miss Carew, when I spoke to Miss Navarro, she told me your aunt was a lady from Cambridge and was painting her portrait. Your aunt wouldn't be a Louisa Brocklehurst, by any chance?'

Vita nodded in reply.

'Bless my soul! I believe I know the lady. Or rather, I did know her years ago. Would she have a moment to catch up with an old friend, do you think? Or would she be too engrossed in her art?'

Never too busy for an old friend, Vita wrote.

'Splendid! Then I shall bid you goodbye with my best wishes for a swift recovery and go immediately to seek out your dear aunt. Let us hope she is in a room warmer than the stables. I nearly froze down there!'

And he left, with a cheerful wave of his hat.

'MISS NAVARRO TELLS me you were pacing the corridors of Crowswood in the middle of the night, Vita. Whatever would Dr Haslam say if he knew?'

Louisa bounced into Vita's room just as the maids were closing the curtains that evening. She had a smear of oil paint on her cheek and the smell of turpentine about her clothing, but looked pleased.

The portrait? Vita wrote.

'All but complete,' her aunt declared, pouring them each a cup of tea from the tray the maid had carried in. 'And though I say it myself, it is one of my best. It may even be *the* best.'

Vita suppressed a smile. She enjoyed the fact that her aunt had no time for false modesty.

'Miss Navarro is a terrible sitter in some ways. She cannot stay still for more than ten minutes at a time, and only gives me an hour's sitting a day. But that apart, she is ideal; unselfconscious, lacking in all vanity, and not even curious about the end result. Once it was settled that I should paint her in her riding clothes, there was no looking back.'

Louisa sipped her tea. A particularly lively look was in her eyes.

'And Vita, imagine this! The veterinary surgeon who came to look at Miss Navarro's prize mare–well done for saving her, by the way–was a dear old friend I had lost touch with, Gully Colindale! Extraordinary! He was a close friend of your uncle's when they were students. They had a great many adventures. They spent a lot of time roving the Norfolk countryside together, steeplechasing and getting into all sorts of scrapes. A dear, dear friend. We lost touch after his wife became ill–oh, it must be a dozen years ago, at least. I heard that she had died, and sent condolences, but I hadn't heard a word since. And then here he is, large as life and twice as cheerful, as they say. Dear old Gulliver. I swear he's worn that same old coat for three decades. But it was marvellous to see him. I have invited him to Eden Street at the earliest opportunity, and he will bring Emily, his daughter. I think of her as a babe in arms, but she is quite the young woman already. He is all for you training as a vet! Did he mention it?'

Vita nodded.

The portrait of Lady Caroline was still propped at the end of the bed. They both looked at it again.

The remains in the basement are those of a man, Vita wrote.

'Yes, some unfortunate workman from years ago, one imagines,' said her aunt. 'Ah, so that's what had you walking about at night. I must say, I should not care to brave those dungeons in the dark myself.'

Wagstaff knows every inch, Vita wrote.

'Wagstaff has gone into hiding,' Louisa said, pouring another cup of tea. 'I really don't know why Consuela puts up with the man. He's normally no more than an arm's length away, but today she rang and rang, but he never appeared. Her maids are very efficient, luckily.'

Perhaps ill? Vita wrote.

'Who knows?' Louisa said. 'The ideal butler is invisible except when needed. He never hovers, he always answers a call immediately, and he never imposes personal difficulties upon the household in any way whatsoever.'

Vita did not reply, but couldn't help thinking butlers would have a hard life, if her aunt were right. *He was helpful last night*, she wrote. *I might seek him out.*

'You will do no such thing. Haslam gave strict instructions that you are to be confined to bed.'

Haslam over-cautious. Vita wrote vigorously. *Younger man like Bennett more modern ideas.*

Her aunt looked puzzled. 'Who is this Bennett? When did a doctor by that name call on you?'

When fever, Vita scribbled.

Her aunt returned both cups and saucers to the tray. 'I must have missed him,' she said. 'Nobody mentioned a Dr Bennett to me.'

A knock was heard at the door before it opened to reveal Wagstaff himself.

'Excuse me, madam. I was wondering if I might have a few words with Miss Carew?'

'Certainly not! She is not to be troubled. My niece has been severely ill. She must rest!' Her aunt told him, in irritation, waving him away with a dismissive flick of her hand.

Wagstaff bowed and began to withdraw, but not before Vita had scrawled *later!* on her pad and held it up while her aunt was looking the other way.

CHAPTER 17

*I*t was after dinner when her father and Edward came to say goodbye. They were leaving in the morning early. Edward had spent the day riding with the Argentinian cattlemen. He was eager to describe his newly acquired skill of lassoing a running steer, but was cut short by his father, who said Vita should not be tired by such stories. Edward wished his sister well, and left her alone with her father.

'There is something important we need to discuss, Vita, now that you are well enough.'

Reverend Carew sat beside the bed. He seemed to search for a way to begin, so Vita wrote, *Mrs Oliver?* on her pad to make it easier.

'Yes, indeed. I imagine your brother or your aunt have said a little to you on the matter. The fact is, Vita, Mrs Oliver has become a dear friend and helper.

We have laboured long and hard together over my little volume on moths of the Devonshire country-side–I must say, it is very pleasing to see it almost complete now–and, well, we have become quite fond of one other.'

He patted his daughter's hand, but did not look directly at her, she noticed. There was a long pause during which her father seemed to struggle with his thoughts, robbed of the power of speech.

Vita was struck by a powerful wave of impatience. She attempted to quell it by counting the crochet points along the edge of her bedsheet. There were twelve. But still her father had not spoken. She wanted to take her pad and write *marriage?* on it (perhaps in capital letters), and have done with this tedious delay, but was aware that her dear Papa was undergoing some sort of inner struggle, and might not appreciate his thoughts being demanded so baldly.

At last the power of speech returned and Rev Carew sat up straight and tapped his daughter's hand in a gesture of new resolution. 'I am considering asking Mrs Oliver... that is to say, if you were to have no objection... I should like to make Mrs Oliver... to ask her to... er... I should like to...

To marry her? Vita wrote it slowly while he watched.

'Precisely!' he said, nodding. 'Nobody will ever replace your dear, dear Mama, of course, but, well, a companion, a helpmate. It would be a comfort, I must confess.'

Vita took his hand and held it. She thought of her dear papa, alone and lonely in his chilly Devon vicarage, and her heart softened. He needed someone.

'Not only that,' her father went on, 'but she has a daughter, Evelyn, close to your own age, a charming girl. You will have a new sister. Well, half-sister. I'm sure you will be the best of friends.'

Vita smiled, trying to conceal how doubtful she felt about that.

'I could not act. I could not dream of asking Mrs Oliver to become my wife without your prior knowledge and approval, Vita. It matters to me a great deal that you too should welcome Agnes and Evelyn into our family.'

Agnes and Evelyn. Vita fought off an instant aversion to the two names, telling herself it was irrational, nonsensical, silly. She nodded her head to indicate something positive to her father, but couldn't think of any words to write.

It was enough for Rev Carew. 'Good! Excellent! So, I shall tell you my plans, Vita. When you are well enough–and there is no hurry about this–you will make your way back to the vicarage. As soon as you are settled and strong enough, the marriage will take place. Mrs Oliver has a large house of her own in Kingsbridge but she is content to leave that to Evelyn, who is shortly to be married to a naval man herself. We shall begin a new life together in the parish. Agnes and I have already planned the next volume of our work on moths, which will involve a certain amount of travelling in the summer months. You will be perfectly comfortable in the vicarage. Your friends will be there. Perhaps a little parish work–people ask after you still. And of course you will be able to keep up with your books and your studies and pursue any other interests in your free time.'

Cambridge? Vita wrote.

'We must accept the inevitable there, I think, Vita.' Her father said. 'It was not meant to be.'

He was looking away, so did not see the shock on his daughter's face. He stood and walked over to the fire.

'Devon has a great deal to offer a young woman with an education. There is no school in the neighbourhood yet. You might consider starting one, though Mrs Oliver was not certain of the need, when I mentioned it. Agnes is of the opinion that you will find your feet, find your mission, so to speak, more easily in your home setting. In Cambridge, everything is so difficult, so competitive. It is an unnatural environment for a young woman of a delicate constitution.'

Vita had never been described as delicate in her life. Her father had many times sent her off into the snowy darkness alone to visit sick parishioners.

Where had this new idea of delicacy suddenly appeared from, she wondered. But then answered herself immediately. From Mrs Agnes Oliver, presumably. Young women were delicate. It was a good reason to keep them at home.

'And besides, Vita, we must be sensible. Our funds are limited. Your brother had a generous bursary, of course, but your fees, well, they have been beyond my reach for some time now. You have exhausted the money your mother left you. It cannot continue. I know you have this little paid post with the Police Surgeon. That is a helpful way of boosting a grant or scholarship, but on its own it would not pay for your books, let alone the disgracefully high fees they charge for scientific instruction. At home in Devon you will be comfortable, your constitution will not be overstrained by study to the extent that you suffer a life-threatening illness such as the one you are recovering from now, and you will be usefully employed among the parishioners and in your new family. Until such time as–well, you don't need me to spell out the possibilities for a young woman's future. Evelyn has a wide circle of friends and she is keen to introduce you to some of her fiancé's naval circle. She is a sociable young woman. You are sure to have happy times, social times, together.'

Vita sank back into her pillows, suppressing a sigh of despair. For a moment, a life of parties and dances with naval gentlemen passed before her eyes. It alternated with memories of long wet walks to poverty-stricken cottages to visit sick people she could only help by offering a few kind words and a little food.

All she could think was, *no. NO!*

But her papa meant well. He was right about their limited funds.

And she had failed the examination.

Her father spoke again. 'Your Aunt Louisa and I have talked at some length about this. She has wrung from me a concession, which is that you should be allowed to stay in Cambridge with her for the time being. I have agreed to this. It is good for Louisa to have company, too. You shall not be hurried. We can wait for you to join us until next summer, if necessary. There. What do you say, Vita?'

Vita blinked, and wrote, *a lot to think over.*

'Indeed,' her father said, standing to leave. 'I will leave you to rest now. We leave early. Write to me, my dear, when you are ready to make arrangements to return.'

He bent to kiss her cheek with warm affection and left.

CHAPTER 18

When Wagstaff knocked and entered later, he found Vita sitting by the fire fully dressed and wearing her coat and boots, which surprised him.

You wanted to see me? she wrote. Then added, *They took the remains?*

The butler was so pale his face appeared grey. His eyes sunken into deep shadows.

'They took what there was. There will be an inquest.' He hung his head. 'I have not told you everything,' he said. 'About what happened when I was a boy here.'

Remains were incomplete, Vita wrote. She was staring into the fire. She pulled her coat closer around her before taking up her notebook again and writing, *more in the icehouse. We should look for ourselves.*

Wagstaff looked astonished as he read these words.

Vita took her pencil and briskly underlined the last sentence she had written. *We should look for ourselves.* Then she stood and pointed to the door.

'Miss Carew, I have a confession.'

Later, she wrote. *Come now. Show me the way.* Without waiting, she sprang out of her chair and walked to the door.

The butler made no move to follow. 'I think I committed a murder,' he said.

But Vita was already on her way.

SPURRED INTO MOVEMENT, Wagstaff caught up with Vita, and led her through the complex knot of dim passageways that seemed unavoidable in the castle. *How is it*, Vita wondered, hurrying after him, *that I never see the same corridor twice?*

Down straight and spiral staircases they descended to the ground floor, emerging into a great entrance hall Vita thought might be the one she had seen when she arrived, but also might not. There were narrow stone passageways, broad panelled landings, and vast echoing chambers, vaulted and timbered high above. There must be some logic to the pattern of rooms in this castle, but Vita had not yet discerned it.

Wagstaff, on the other hand, moved with the familiarity of a rat in its burrow.

I know nothing about this man, and yet I follow him into the darkest recesses of this shadowy place. Perhaps I am as deluded as Mrs Oliver thinks I am, Vita thought. *It would be so much more prudent and sensible to stay by the nice, warm fire in my room.*

They rounded a corner. Another stuffed crow leaned to glare at them from among the roof beams.

Sensible! My whole life will be prudent and sensible when I return to Devon. Prudent, sensible and, of course, sociable. Let's not forget the naval gentlemen!

'Miss Carew, it is this way,' Wagstaff's voice interrupted her thoughts. She had missed a turn.

At some point, Wagstaff equipped himself with a coat and a lantern–he carried no light inside the castle–and led Vita out, across a driveway, and onto the grass of the park. They walked for what seemed a long time. The route led up a slope away from the castle and through a coppice of trees still dripping from the earlier rain.

It is a long way to this icehouse, Vita thought. *Surely this would be an inconvenient distance to haul blocks of ice?*

'It is on the north side of this bank,' Wagstaff said. 'The cold side. There is a cart track, but it goes round the back, out of sight of the castle.'

They rounded a shoulder of the hill and Wagstaff

showed her the cart track. It was recently used, and muddy. Off to one side, there were signs of digging. Mounds of earth were piled aside.

'The men are making a wider track up here. A new carriage drive to the top of the hill for the view. They were the ones who found the icehouse. The entrance has been overgrown for years.'

He lifted the lantern so that it shone into the dark mouth of what looked to Vita like a cave. A few feet inside, a barred metal gate spanned the whole width. Even just inside the arched brickwork entrance, the air felt noticeably colder. It had the permanent clammy chill of a place never warmed by sunlight, even at the height of summer. The natural human response was to turn away. Leave. Find a warm dry place with light that did not smell of dead leaves, mildew, rot.

Wagstaff led Vita as far as the gate, raising his lantern so that it lit the vaulted brickwork beyond. It was a broad dome, except that at the far end, the quality of darkness was different and bricks littered the floor.

'That's where they broke in,' Wagstaff told her. 'They said there was a hole in the roof already, and they made it bigger. Climbed down for a look.'

Wagstaff held the light, but made no move to enter beyond the iron gate.

Where were remains? Vita wrote, pulling her notebook from her pocket.

'Just here, behind the gate,' Wagstaff said. He turned away, suddenly pressing his back against the railings. 'I cannot go in, Miss. I will not set foot in this accursed place. I haven't the stomach for it.' His face was livid in the lantern's wavering light. He touched his forehead and his knees gave way. Vita saw the light lurch as Wagstaff crumpled and fell to the ground. The lantern hit the damp ground and went out. Darkness enveloped them.

'WAGSTAFF?' Vita heard her own voice, an unfamiliar croaking whisper, echo in the dome of the icehouse.

After a moment of blinking in the darkness, she groped for the railings, the chill creeping further into her bones. A slurry of mud and leaf mould squelched under her boots, its mushroom smell tainted–perhaps it was only her imagination–with the underlying hint of putrefaction.

Outside the icehouse, wind lashed the leafless trees and a thin but penetrating rain fell, its insistent hiss the only other sound.

Vita turned and looked out of the entrance tunnel. There was light enough in the distant sky only to make out the churning of wind-whipped branches. A small pale shape, like a handkerchief caught in the wind, moved in the distance. It seemed to be approaching. Vita shuddered.

A groan, a movement. Wagstaff. He needed help.

It was tempting to run to the castle and raise the alarm. Anything that took her out of this place and into the company of living beings was strongly appealing, but Vita could not bring herself to leave Wagstaff alone when he was so clearly terrified. Whatever he feared had frightened him into a swoon, perhaps even a heart attack.

She fell to her hands and knees and groped for the lantern, finding it by its residual heat and the smell of its spilled oil. It was not broken, but she had no matches to relight it, so could only set it upright and feel her way over to the fallen butler. She found his shoulder and an arm in the darkness and put her hand to his chest, reassured to feel the movement of a beating heart beneath her palm. It was too fast, but at least it had not stopped.

'Wagstaff? Can you hear me?'

In first aid classes, the advice had been to lift an unconscious person into a sitting position. Wagstaff had fallen close to the railings, so she would only have to pull him upright to lean him against them. She hauled on his coat and he groaned. He was regaining consciousness. His head straightened, and he mumbled. She couldn't make out his words, but they seemed urgent.

Leaning back to catch her breath, Vita glimpsed the fluttering pale shape again, larger this time, beyond the mouth of the icehouse.

'Matches. Have you any matches?' she asked him.

He moved to pat one of his coat pockets and Vita plunged her hand unceremoniously into it and found them.

Relighting the lamp would not be easy. Its oil had spilled. There might not be enough left for it to burn, and striking a match in this windy tunnel seemed hopeless, too. Vita groped for it anyway and fumbled the matchbox open. Three matches.

The first took several strikes before it even attempted to give a flame, but melted to smoke long before Vita could put it to the lantern. She held the second one much closer, but that refused to strike at all.

'Allow me, Miss, if you please. I know these matches.' Wagstaff was awake enough to be watching.

Vita felt towards him and handed him the match-box, relieved that it would be the butler and not her who had to try the last match.

'Stay there, Miss. You can shelter me from the wind.'

She heard movement but could see nothing until the characteristic scratch of a match's head against a matchbox was followed by a tiny flash of flame and after a pause, during which she held her breath, by the hiss and sputter of an oil lamp lighting. The light, which had seemed dim and inadequate before, was so welcome now that both grinned as its soft glow rose around them.

'Are you unwell?' Vita asked. 'You collapsed.'

'I don't know what happened. I fainted, perhaps. This place holds everything I fear most.'

'Human remains, do you mean?'

'Secrets,' Wagstaff said. 'Secrets I have carried with me my whole life long.'

'We should return to the castle. I should ask them to send for Dr Haslam. There may be something wrong with your heart. You need to be examined. It is not good for you to stay here in the cold. Come, I will hold the lantern. We can be back indoors in a few minutes.'

'Please, miss. It will be worse for me if we do not finish looking here. I believe I know what we will find. It is only just here, behind the gate.'

'Find what?'

'The remaining parts of the body, and what goes with it.'

Vita lifted the lantern. Just on the other side of the gate, there was a pile of leaves, mud and debris that had obviously been disturbed. Presumably this was where the workmen had dug out the remains she had seen in the castle. It had been roughly done. Someone with a spade and the urgent desire to get the remains shifted as quickly as possible had left a considerable remainder untouched. It looked like rotted leaves, earth, and a few muddied rags.

'Is this gate locked?' Vita pulled on it without effect.

'I have the key.' Wagstaff drew a large key from his pocket, turning it hesitantly over in his hand several times before holding it out to Vita.

CHAPTER 19

*V*ita slid the key into the lock, but could not make it turn. She looked helplessly at Wagstaff, who struggled to his feet and tried it himself. This time the key turned in the lock quite easily. Rusted hinges squealed loudly as it swung open, the sound triggering a skittering of rats in the dark interior.

'I cannot go in,' Wagstaff said.

'Just hold the lantern,' Vita told him, brisk in her impatience to get this over with.

The pile of rags was not as soft as rags and earth alone should be. Vita crouched and plunged her hand into it, pushing the earth aside. Some parts crumbled and fell away. But there were clotted clumps of sticky earth too, and pushing on one of those revealed a pale irregular shape. It was white in the lantern light. A scapula.

The light trembled as Wagstaff watched in silence from the other side of the gate. He clutched the railings.

Vita knelt beside the pile of earth now topped by the knuckle of the shoulder bone. She scooped earth and pieces of sodden fabric away on either side. After several minutes, the rest of an arm was revealed down the wrist.

'The hand?' Wagstaff breathed through the bars. 'Is the hand there?'

It was. Vita dug more slowly now, well aware of the complexity of the wrist joint. One by one, each of the connecting bones was revealed until she pulled out the fine bones of the thumb. The other finger bones were disordered and wedged into the soil. She dug further, finding them here and there until something caught the light. A gold signet ring, still encircling the lower joint of the fourth finger.

Vita was fastidious about the treatment of these bones. She followed the method she had observed in the Police Surgeon's laboratory, placing each in order carefully to one side, to reveal where something was missing. She was so preoccupied with this thorough procedure that the sound of Wagstaff's gasp only registered with her gradually.

'The ring. May I see it?'

It was muddy, but she extracted it and handed it to him through the railings of the gate.

'It is his,' Wagstaff said. 'See the crow? It is his.

The Earl's. This must be him. He must have been here all along. It is just as I feared. Oh, God forgive me. God forgive me, please. I was a child. I did not know.'

Laid on the brickwork floor, the skeletal remains of the hand and arm were now complete. As Vita stood up to see what Wagstaff could mean, a figure rushed in at the icehouse entrance. Her hair was loose and wet, flying around her pale face, her clothes bedraggled and damp.

'Is it him?' the woman cried. 'Is it? Is it?'

The woman pressed herself frantically against the railings, grasping them with pale hands, then turned and pointed a trembling finger at the butler. 'The ring. Is that the ring, Wagstaff?'

'It is,' Wagstaff answered. He handed the woman the ring. She took it and held it on the palm of her hand up to the light of the lantern, turning it to peer at the crow engraved in the black amber of the seal.

'It is,' she said. 'It is Mountfitchet. We have him at last, Wagstaff. At last.' She said these words quietly, her tone one of relief, of release, even.

'I killed him. I locked the gate. I did not know, Lady Caroline. I did not know. I swear it on my life,' Wagstaff put his head in his hands, sobbing.

The pale lady put a hand to Wagstaff's shoulder. She looked a moment longer at the ring, then spoke gently. 'You must not allow him to break you,

Wagstaff. Not now, after all these years. You are a brave man. You must find your courage,' she said.

Something had puzzled Vita, something familiar about the woman she now watched studying the ring. And then the connection fell into place and she recognised this pale lady as the strange night nurse who had visited her room when she was ill.

'Lady Caroline? You are Lady Caroline from the painting?' she asked.

'I am a great deal older than that now, Dear,' the lady said, as if it were necessary to explain. 'I am glad to see you looking better, but you should not be in this cold place for too long, if I may say so.'

'I thought you were dead,' Vita said.

'Not dead, Dear. Just mad, and sent away. But I am back now. I am still a little mad, aren't I Wagstaff? But only a little. And nobody minds.'

'Lady Caroline lives in a cottage in the grounds,' Wagstaff said.

'She should not be out in her nightgown on a night like this,' Vita told him. 'Wagstaff, you should take her home.'

'I shall,' he said. He stood. Removing his overcoat, he wrapped it round Lady Caroline's shoulders. 'I shall walk you home, now, Milady.'

He lifted the lantern high, throwing its light further into the back of the icehouse.

'What was that?' Vita asked. 'I saw something at the back.'

'There are bound to be rats, Miss,' Wagstaff said uneasily.

'No, it was not a rat. I saw something else. A shape. Hold the lantern higher, Wagstaff, just for a moment. If it is something, we can send someone else to look, or come back ourselves tomorrow, but I want to see what it is before we leave.'

Vita stepped carefully across the damp and slippery brickwork towards the curved wall at the back. Over to her right was the pile of fallen bricks where the workmen had pushed their way in, but on the left…

The muddy outline of the object lying there in the sodden leaves and rat litter was familiar. Vita picked it up, turned, and held it to the lantern's fading light. It was a shoe. As she peered at it, a clot of leaves peeled away and fell to the ground, revealing its colour, a mottled but unmistakable kingfisher blue. The lantern guttered and gave out, plunging them all into darkness.

'ABSURD!' Louisa was saying, when Vita woke the next morning. 'Quite, quite ridiculous! Whose idea was it? If it was that butler's, I shall see to it that he is given his marching orders immediately. You have been dangerously ill, and there you are traipsing about in the middle of the night in some damp and dangerous ice house! Apart from anything else, the whole thing might have collapsed on you. I only hope you have not caught your death of cold. Wait until I tell Dr Haslam! He will have something to say about these night wanderings, I can tell you!'

'I feel quite well, Aunt...' Vita started to say.

'No! Don't speak! You must not exert your vocal cords, remember. Vita, you are a truly dreadful patient. We shall have to chain you to the bedstead! And handling a dead body that has lain untouched for decades! What were you thinking?'

'Two dead bodies, as a matter of fact.'

'I beg your pardon?'

'There are two sets of remains in the icehouse.'

Her aunt fell into the chair by the bedside, shaking her head. 'Oh my word, what a place this is!'

'I met Lady Caroline last night,' Vita said, nodding towards the portrait still set at the end of the bed.

'You met this lady? Isn't she long dead?'

'Not at all. She is older, obviously, but quite energetic. She lives in a cottage in the grounds.'

'Why ever did nobody mention that?'

'We assumed she was dead. Nobody told us she was'

'You shouldn't speak, Vita. Where is your notebook?'

'She visited me when I was sick, but I was so feverish I thought she was a night nurse.'

145

'She crept into your bedroom at night? Oh, dear me! This place is chaos. We shall certainly be leaving as soon as Haslam says you are well enough to travel.'

'Have you seen Wagstaff this morning?' Vita asked.

'No! Dreadful man involving you in all this nonsense! I have been putting the final touches to the portrait until I was interrupted by Consuela telling me a complicated story about you and the butler searching the icehouse in the middle of the night. I could hardly believe my ears, except that the tale was so ridiculous it was beyond fantasy! I'm only glad your father and brother left early and missed hearing about all this. Goodness only knows what your father would make of it. He would be beside himself!'

Vita was relieved to have avoided her father's disapproval. 'Father told me his plans to marry Mrs Oliver. I expect he told you,' she said.

'He did.' Her aunt nodded her head, but avoided Vita's eye.

'I am to live in the vicarage and help with parish work.'

'He thinks it best,' said her aunt. 'He wants you settled in your life, and happy.'

'Perhaps it is for the best,' Vita said. 'I failed the examination. I seem to have no great gift for scientific study.'

They both concentrated on the pattern of the bedcover for a few moments.

'I convinced him to allow you to complete this academic year, at least.'

'Thank you for that, Aunt. I am truly sorry to have caused you so much worry.'

Her aunt patted her hand. 'Do not speak, Dear! How many times must I remind you?'

CHAPTER 20

*I*t was Wagstaff himself who carried in her luncheon tray. Maria followed, fussed over the patient's pillows, and offered to feed her the soup.

Vita shook her head. 'I can do it myself, thank you Maria,' she said, 'and I wonder, could I have something other than soup? The soup is quite marvellous, but is there something different I could try? Something soft?'

Maria left to find something.

Wagstaff busied himself tending to the fire. 'I hope you are recovered, Wagstaff. You said last night that you had a confession to make,' Vita said, 'but events overtook us. Would you feel able to tell me now?'

'Quite able,' he replied briskly. 'I told Miss Navarro this morning. I no longer have any secrets.'

He seemed different. The same short and serious-faced butler, but there was a subtly different air about him. A weight lifted, perhaps. He came to the bedside and refilled Vita's water glass.

'Please sit down,' Vita said, 'and tell me what you can.'

He sat. A seated butler. It still seemed strange to both of them. 'I hardly know where to start,' he said.

'From the beginning, if you please,' Vita told him.

'Well,' he said, 'I told you before, I think, that I am an orphan. I was born and lived my first years in the workhouse in Dereham. The old butler, Mr Warren, took me on here as a kitchen boy when I was ten years old. I was not too much beaten or bullied. I liked it here. Only,' he paused and ran his hand over his mouth, 'only, the master, Mountfitchet, was a very cruel man.

'We all knew it. There was nothing the staff could do, of course. We just had to lump it and keep out of his way, but the castle was full of nastiness. Drunken brawls and misconduct of all sorts. Nobody down-stairs was happy. Some left, but most had nowhere to go. They'd been here for years, for generations, some of them. Anyway, the Earl married Lady Caroline and he brought her back to Crowswood and some of the staff thought it might settle him down, being married, but they were wrong about that.

'He was cruel to Lady Caroline from the start. He never cared for her. She was young, and she was a bit, well, she was not strong in her head, we could see that. It was easy to scare her, and he did. He spent her money, as much as he could get his hands on, and then he wanted her taken away to an asylum so he could have the rest. We watched it all happen. It was wrong, but what could we do? Anyone who stood up to him was thrown out without a reference, and that meant being on the streets, hungry.

'And then–I told you this part–I was up one morning early and I saw a lady in a blue dress lying dead at the foot of the great staircase. And the Earl came and moved her, carried her body away and hid it in a cupboard. And later the body was gone when I looked. And nobody ever spoke about it, even though Lady Caroline was on the stairs that morning and saw the dead lady for herself.

'Nobody spoke of it. But I had the shoe. I kept the shoe.

He sighed. 'You know this. But you don't know the next part. I ran errands, carried things, hauled coal and slops and pig food, but I was most often in the kitchen, and I was always listening. I heard the staff complain about the Earl and his drunken, horrible friends day in and day out. They hated what he did.

His father had led a quiet country life. They had respected him. This young Earl they despised. In particular, they hated the way he treated Lady Caroline. He beat her and cursed her without caring who heard. He was in and out of other ladies' rooms. The servants knew all about it. Every nasty detail. He wanted Lady Caroline rid of to the asylum, and he paid people to scare her–it isn't difficult to scare someone in this dark and gloomy old place–and she was a timid lady, easily frightened. He drove her to madness.

'I heard them mutter about him. I saw footmen and maids come back to the kitchen, pale and trembling with rage over the way he behaved to his young wife.

He stretched his shoulders. 'In all honesty, Miss, I was so young that there were a lot of things I gave up trying to understand. Crowswood was my world, but it wasn't a place that made sense. Lady Caroline was sent away quite soon after the lady in blue died. All we knew was that she was bundled into a carriage and driven away. We didn't know where she'd been sent to at first, but then instructions came to forward her things, and we knew he had put her in the lunatic asylum in Garston Lacey.

'After she was gone, Crowswood got worse. While the Earl was here, it was mayhem, drunken parties, gambling, crowds of his friends, all sorts of bad behaviour. The staff dreaded the sight of his carriage on the drive. He arrived and left without notice. He left his guests here sometimes, without a word of explanation. He had other houses and nobody to stop him from coming and going as he pleased.

'Then one day, Warren, the old butler, took me aside. He called me into his pantry–I'd never set foot in there before–it was like heaven to me. A big fire, a comfortable armchair. I should like to be a butler myself one day, I thought. But I never really dreamed it could be. I was nothing, after all. But Mr Warren, he sat me down and he said, *Billy, I have a favour to ask you, and if you do it right, I shall see to it that one day this room is yours. You will never have to worry about making a living because you will be a proper, trained-up butler and comfortable here in the castle for the rest of your days. Would you like that, Billy?*

'I said I would like it with all my heart. He made me buttered toast on his own fire, and he told me what he wanted me to do.

'It was an easy thing. All I had to do was wait to be called, and when someone told me it was time, I should go out to the icehouse–they would show me the way–and I was to lock the gate. And after that, I should never tell anyone about it.

'I said I'd do it. Of course I did. And he said it might be soon or I might have to wait a while, but he would let me know when the time came. And the most important part of all was not to tell anyone, not anyone, ever.

'So I never did. I was eleven years old then, and I have never told a living soul until this morning, when I told Miss Navarro. And now I am telling you.'

Vita looked past the butler at the fire, which was a good blaze. Maria had entered at some point and carried in another tray.

'You locked the icehouse gate, as they told you to?'

'Yes.'

'They didn't ask you to do anything else?'

'Only to return the key to Warren, and never mention doing it.'

'But why did they want you to do it?'

'At the time, I hardly even wondered. I just did as I was told because I wanted to stay here, to be safe here, to have a home. Over the years, I told myself the lady in blue had been put in the icehouse after she died. Hidden there. And they wanted it locked so nobody would find her body.'

'But once I told you the remains the workmen found in the icehouse were *male*…'

Wagstaff closed his eyes and sighed, shaking his head. 'I knew then that I must have been wrong all along. A horrible suspicion took hold of my thoughts. And when you found the ring, there was no doubt left. That signet ring with the crow on it belonged to the Earl himself. The body must be his. All these years he's lain there. And it was I who locked him in.'

Vita looked at the butler, searching his face for the truth.

'You truly didn't know?'

'I just went and locked the gate, as I was told. I was eleven years old. It was a dark night. Mr Warren walked me over there and I locked the gate and gave the key back to him.'

'And nobody ever mentioned it again?'

'No.'

They looked at one another, the butler's story seeming to hang in the air between them.

'May I ask you a few more questions, Wagstaff? It is not too unpleasant?'

'I would be glad if you did. I want only to make sense of it. It has haunted me for so long.'

'How could anyone have succeeded in getting the Earl into the icehouse? It was derelict even then, you said?'

'It was. It was overgrown. You could hardly tell it was there. But getting him there would be easy enough. He was a heavy drinker. I often heard footmen complain about having to carry him to his bed dead drunk. They joked about it. Said they could easily drop him down the stairs, or push him out of a window, and he'd never even know.'

'But it would not be the work of one person to move him? Not right out to the icehouse.'

'No. They could use the cart, but it'd still need two or three. And as butler, Mr Warren held all the keys. He'd have to open the gate.'

'So it would have to be a conspiracy? The staff would have to agree a plan. Were the staff, as far as you remember, in close enough agreement to do that?'

'They all agreed the Earl was wrong to treat his wife the way he did. They complained of it constantly in the kitchen. Mr Warren hated what the master did to Lady Caroline.'

'Enough to make a secret plan with others to kill him?'

'They saw every detail. They knew every nasty thing he did. I believe they did truly hate him.'

'But why didn't they hurl him out of a window instead of locking him into the icehouse? It would have looked like an accident.'

Wagstaff looked away. 'It wasn't enough. That would be my guess.'

'Enough in what way?'

The butler paused and ran his hand over his mouth before continuing. 'They wanted him to suffer. I don't think they wanted a quick or easy end for the man who had shamed his family's name and forced his innocent wife into an asylum. They wanted revenge. He was a nervous man, the Earl. Especially after Lady Caroline was sent away. He never spent a night in the castle on his own. He filled it with guests, but it wasn't just because he loved company, it was because he hated to be alone here. He kept candles burning all night. He made footmen sleep outside his door. He had terrified his poor wife with stories, but it was he who was afraid of ghosts. Or a bit mad. I don't know for sure. I only heard kitchen talk, but it was always joked about, that he was scared of the dark, of the shadows. That he saw things move and heard strange noises and voices calling to him at night.

'They must have waited until he was dead drunk, carried him out to the icehouse, and left him in there in the dark, knowing he would be terrified out of his wits when he woke up. They wanted to give him a taste of his own medicine.'

'But why go to the trouble of having you, the kitchen boy, turn the key?'

'I have spent many, many hours wondering,' Wagstaff said. 'It seems to me there are two main possibilities. Firstly, the staff agreed the plan to rid themselves of the Earl together, but nobody wanted to carry out the final act–locking him in–because that would make them the killer. If all of them together took a small part, and the locking of the gate was done by an innocent child, then no one person could be held responsible.'

'It sounds very elaborate,' Vita said.

'You shouldn't under-estimate the ingenuity or the dedication of the people who worked here in the castle. They had a lot of time on their hands when the master was away. They were driven on by anger at the way Lady Caroline was treated. They had watched his cruelty towards her for several years and seen a gentle young woman broken by what he did to her.'

'It is hard to believe, even so.'

'Not for me. I saw how their lives were distorted by the Earl and the way he lived. They were good people. For them, it was against the natural order of things that a powerful man, a nobleman from a family that had been honourable in the past, should be such a cruel and drunken wastrel.'

'So they were righting a great wrong?'

'In their eyes, yes.'

'But why involve you?'

'Well, as I said, it kept each of them from having to commit the final act.'

He looked up at her quite sharply then. 'But there is something else. It occurred to me only last night.'

'What did?'

Wagstaff looked away quickly. 'It is just something that occurred to me. I need to look into it further.'

'Another mystery?'

'Another possible explanation.'

Vita could only shake her head. It was a great deal to take in.

Maria, who had waited, brought over a tray. A dish of soft poached egg glistened on it. 'Is enough,' Maria said firmly to Wagstaff. 'Lady must eat and rest. You go.' She dismissed the butler with a flick of her hand.

A maid dismissing a butler, Vita thought, as she watched Wagstaff leave. Revolutions on every side!

CHAPTER 21

$\mathcal{W}$hen Vita woke in the night, she was surprised to make out a figure in the soft light of the fading fire across the room. It was Dr Bennett sitting in the fireside chair. He was staring into the flickering embers.

'I am surprised to find you here,' Vita said. 'I have not had a fever for several days now. There is no need for you to keep watch over me, Dr Bennett.'

The doctor did not move or seem to hear. He continued to stare into the fireplace, holding his hands up to warm them at the dying fire. 'I am cold,' he said, after a long pause.

'Please, put some more wood on the fire. Build it up, if you feel the cold,' Vita told him.

Without moving or looking round, Bennett continued to rub his hands and stretch them into the fireplace. He did this for several long minutes, before standing. Picking up his medical bag, he placed it on a side table and removed a tubular carrying case from which he withdrew several long-handled medical instruments.

'We discussed your surgery, Miss Dean. Do you remember?' he said. He laid a cloth from his medical bag on the table and placed the instruments in a row upon it, then carefully removed his black jacket and began to roll the sleeves of his shirt. Each movement was performed with slow deliberation. He appeared completely absorbed in his own actions.

Vita had no explanation for his behaviour. She could only wonder whether the young man was playing a trick on her. 'Doctor Bennett, I am not Miss Dean. I am Vita Carew, remember? You have been treating me for a throat infection and fever.'

He gave no sign of hearing this. 'There will be some pain, it is unavoidable,' he said, 'but I shall carry out the procedure as quickly as I can. It will soon be over.'

When the doctor turned he was holding up an ebony handled silver scalpel. He approached the bed, saying, 'Hold Miss Dean's shoulders and arms, if you please.'

'There's nobody here, Doctor Bennett. Nobody but me,' Vita told him. His remote, unseeing, unhearing manner was disturbing her now. His movements were strange too, halting and unnatural, like a faltering sleep walker.

'There is no alternative. I must operate immediately,' he said.

The chill the doctor had complained of had now filled the room. Vita felt her muscles clench against its sudden presence. She shivered. Looking up at the young doctor, she saw that his eyes were focused elsewhere, as if he were seeing someone else on the bed. He leaned toward her, the scalpel outstretched.

As Vita drew away from him, the door opened, and they were joined in the room by the silver grey figure of Lady Caroline.

'My dear, I hope you will not mind a visit at this late hour?' she asked. She fluttered in wearing her usual costume of lacey grey, complete with long grey gloves, but paused when she saw the figure standing over the bed.

'Does he trouble you, Miss Carew? This young man? He visits a little too often, perhaps? You find him a little too persistent?'

'He insists that I am a Miss Dean, and that I need urgent surgery,' Vita said, still pressed back in her pillows as the scalpel hovered above her.

'You are getting carried away again, Bennett. Your patient is perfectly well,' the old lady said, raising her voice as if the young doctor were hard of hearing. She turned back to Vita. 'He is no trouble, really, except that he is inclined to linger a little too long. And then he starts with the *procedures*. He leaves if you ask him to. But you see, he won't listen to me. It has to be you, the patient, who sends him away.'

'I don't understand,' Vita said.

The doctor had not moved, he still seemed intent on deploying his scalpel.

'It is nothing to worry about. Just tell him to leave, and he will go.'

Vita found everything about this explanation strange, but she certainly felt inclined to remove the doctor, if she could. 'I am quite recovered now, thank you, Dr Bennett,' she told him. When he made no move, she repeated her words more commandingly. 'Dr Bennett, I no longer require your treatment.'

The doctor hesitated, then let his hands fall to his sides and stepped away from the bedside to return to the fire. He stood looking at the blaze with his back towards them. His long brown hair hung over the collar of his jacket.

Lady Caroline shook her head. 'You will need to tell him to go quite firmly,' she said. 'They rarely take a hint, in my experience.'

'They?'

'Just send him away, my dear.'

Vita looked towards the doctor across the dim bedroom again. The shadows were closing in around him. 'You must go now, Dr Bennett,' she said more assertively, adding, 'but thank you for all you have done.'

And somehow he was no longer there.

Vita peered across the room, confused. Her own hands suddenly felt very cold.

'There is no harm in him,' Lady Caroline told her with a reassuring smile. 'There is really no harm in any of them. The Earl could never understand. He was always fussing and fretting. Once he had people come from a society for some sort of research! They had a high old time. It was a lot of bother, if I remember. Of course, they didn't listen to me. Nobody ever does. I could have told them that if you are clear and definite, they generally leave you alone. They mean well, on the whole. Though there are one or two exceptions.'

'I think I saw a child of the same sort too.'

'Yes, yes. He and the child both come and go. Miss Dean was a patient of the young doctor's. They both met a sad end. He cut himself on a glass, I believe. Caught an infection. Blood poisoning or some such thing.'

Questions crowded into Vita's mind, but she sensed that Lady Caroline would not welcome or answer them. 'Could you tell me about the portrait, Lady Caroline?' she asked, changing the subject with relief to something more tangible.

They both looked at the portrait, still standing at the end of the bed.

'Well, of course, Dear, of course! It was painted in Garston Lacey.'

'The asylum?'

'Yes. People shudder when you say the word, but it was not a bad place. Most of the staff were kind. I made good friends there. One of them, Sebastian, was a painter. He painted my picture for something to do. We were always finding little projects for ourselves. We thought it would be entertaining–a little riddle–to paint a few secrets into it. I never imagined Mountfitchet would hang it over the fireplace for everyone to see, but he did. He loved the crows, I suppose, and never stopped to wonder what any of it meant. Nobody did.'

'My aunt and I wondered. Well, my aunt is a painter, and she felt there was something odd about it. And when I was ill, I had a lot of time to look at it.'

'And what did you find?'

Vita pointed to the painting. 'The big crow must represent Mountfitchet and the small one could be you. The small one in a cage because you were confined there at Garston Lacey. Is that correct?'

'Yes, quite correct.'

'And the kingfisher?'

'Oh dear, yes, the poor kingfisher. He painted it well, I think.'

'He painted it very well, but why did he put a

dead kingfisher in the claw of the Mountfitchet crow?'

'Oh dear, it is very sad. So very sad. I told him to do that. I saw something bad, you see. I tried to tell people, but they wouldn't listen to me.'

'Can you tell me what you saw?'

Lady Caroline touched a finger to the blue of the kingfisher in the painting. 'Such a colour!' she said. 'Beautiful, don't you agree?'

'Yes, it is a wonderful colour.'

'I saw him push her. Push her over the banister. A lady in a dress of this colour. They quarrelled. She was a small woman, but she was angry. He had been drinking. Something she said irked him and he pushed her. She tumbled against the banister, her arms flew open, and she just fell. I can see it now, even as I say the words. It was over in a second. A scream and a terrible crack. She hit the flagstone floor.'

Lady Caroline frowned and shook her head. 'I have seen it, dreamt it, thought about it a thousand times. Could I have done something? Shouted? Saved her? I should perhaps have tried, but I did nothing at the time. It happened so very quickly.'

She shook her head and pressed her lips with her gloved fingers. 'It was after one of his long nights. I had been to bed. I never joined them. But I heard something in the early morning and came out of my room. This room, as it happens. And I saw it happen. Poor, poor creature. He killed her.'

'Did you not speak of it?'

'Nobody listened to me. He had me taking medicines, powders and syrups that made me sleepy and muddled my thoughts even more than they muddle themselves. I could hardly tell if it was day or night. At Garston Lacey, I was free of all that. My thoughts were clearer. I began to trust myself again. That was when I knew it was true. So when Sebastian painted this, I asked him to show what I knew. He did it beautifully, poor Sebastian. He was quite mad, but he was a gentle young man, and talented. He painted the dead kingfisher to represent the lady, and he showed the same blue in my eyes, and in the small crow's eyes to tell people that I saw what happened to her.'

'Who was the lady in the blue dress? Do you know?'

'His guests were nearly all strangers to me. I might have seen her at dinner, but I certainly never knew her name. She was one of his special friends, I imagine. Poor thing.'

'I think her remains are in the ice house along with Mountfitchet's.'

The old lady looked calm at this news, but said thoughtfully, 'She died some time before he left, though.'

'Wagstaff thinks the staff waited until the master was dead drunk and then locked him in the icehouse with the remains of her dead body.'

The old lady's fingers pulled at the buttons on one of her long gloves for a moment.

'He was in fear all his life of the dark, of death, of hauntings and ghosts,' Lady Caroline said. 'To be locked in the cold darkness with his own poor victim's corpse would be everything terrible he could imagine all at once. If that is true, I pity him.'

CHAPTER 22

*W*hen her aunt entered the following morning, Vita was already dressed and writing in her notebook.

'It is marvellous to see you up and looking so well, Dear, but has Dr Haslam given permission?'

'I have given my own permission,' Vita said.

'He will call later, anyway, and with luck, you will be allowed to travel. We can get back to Eden Street and a normal existence that does not include corpses in icehouses. I, for one, shall not be sorry to leave Crowswood behind,' her aunt declared.

'Miss Navarro has seen the portrait?'

'She has seen it. She is delighted with it, and she has paid me in full. She will call in to see you later. She is out with the horses. The foal you helped to deliver is thriving, by the way.'

'Would she mind if I explored the castle while I wait for the doctor?'

'Not at all, I'm sure. Edward and your father enjoyed wandering around when they were here, but you must wear a coat. The cold in most of the rooms is arctic. I'll stay in my room by the fire, if you don't mind. I have letters to write.'

VITA, well-wrapped in a hat, scarf and gloves, set off to explore the castle, marvelling over the difference in its atmosphere in daylight. Dank and gloomy passages still led off into darkness here and there, but she avoided them and, keeping to the wider corridors, soon rediscovered the strange gallery displaying the hunting trophies and Mountfitchet's extensive collection of stuffed crows. In the daylight they were still unpleasant, but many had a moth-eaten shabbiness that made them more pitiful than terrifying.

A vast set of double doors led off on the far side, so she stepped away from the stares of the glass-eyed birds and beasts and went to see what was there. Her hand was on the elaborate handle of the door when Wagstaff's voice spoke behind her.

'I see you have found the library,' he said.

'Is it a good one?'

'I couldn't tell you,' he said, coming over to join

her. 'I have never seen another. You must judge that for yourself.'

He opened the doors with a flourish and revealed a cavernous room. It was as large as college libraries Vita had seen in Cambridge. Spiral iron stairways led up bookcases that, in some places, were twenty feet high. Every space on the shelves was filled. Some of the books seemed ancient, but others were evidently more modern. It was not a dusty museum of untouched antique books, it had the air of being used, cared for, and even stocked with newer publications. Large tables with glowing reading lamps were scatted with volumes, some of them open, as if readers were at work.

'Miss Navarro uses this place? It seems well-visited,' Vita remarked.

'It is,' Wagstaff said. 'But there is only one reader, and that is myself.'

'So this is how you passed the time,' Vita said. She wandered into the room, glancing at the open books on the table. There was an atlas, there were books about astronomy and one about Egyptian history. Open on the other side was a collection of Elizabethan sonnets and a biography of Canaletto.

'This is my university,' he said, holding up his arms. 'After Cook taught me to read from recipe books, I crept in here whenever I could. In all the years the castle was empty, I had this library all to myself. I read whatever took my fancy. I have had no teachers and no schooling, but I have been able to read.'

'This is a fine place. A fine university,' Vita said.

He smiled. 'Please,' he said, 'make yourself at home.'

Vita wasted no time in exploring the shelves. Previous Earls of Mountfitchet had equipped their library with most of the great works of Europe, it seemed. Grand leather-bound volumes, their spines elegantly tooled in gold, lined the shelves. History and the classics were well served, but there was little on the subject of science, although there was a collection of volumes about engineering and architecture in an alcove.

Vita wandered the shelves, exploring the collection and imagining the glory of having a grand library all to herself.

In a dim corner shelf against the far wall, a shelf of plainly bound volumes with dates hand written on the spine caught her eye. They stood out from the other books for their functional binding. Vita lifted one down and found it was a ledger.

'Those are just the old household account books. Mr Warren left them in the butler's pantry. I brought them here to the library because they took up too much space.'

'The household accounts?' Vita asked. She was looking at a page of careful columned entries recording the purchase of kitchen goods, candles, wax paper, lye, sugar, salt, with the prices, quantities and sellers' names. Every entry was itemised in an elaborate copperplate script.

'And what are these?' Vita asked, indicating a shelf of smaller, more handsomely bound volumes, also dated along the spine.

'Visitor's books,' he said. 'It was common for guests to write some little quip or message along with their name as they left.'

'I suppose, if we are seeking the lady in blue, she will not be in there, since she never did leave,' Vita said thoughtfully.

Wagstaff looked at her, suddenly alert. 'She might have visited on a previous occasion. Many of his guests did return.'

Vita took two or three of the visitor's books off the shelf and carried them to a table. 'With your permission,' she said, 'I should like to look through these visitor's books, and see whether there's a Mimi among the signatures. It does not seem likely, but perhaps it's worth a half hour's effort.'

'My permission?' Wagstaff looked at her quickly, wondering if he was being mocked. 'As butler, I have no real business here in the library. You, as a guest, have the perfect right to examine any volume you please.'

'Thank you,' she said. 'But you said this place is also your university, so I did not want to intrude.'

171

'What I said seems ridiculous to you, no doubt,' Wagstaff said, stiffly.

'Ridiculous? No! It seems wholly admirable,' Vita told him. 'But it must have been a hard, and above all, a solitary pursuit. I find my own studies difficult enough, but I am surrounded by teachers and other students. Talking with them is the enjoyable part of learning. Perhaps I hadn't appreciated that before. Ideas are sparked and flourish easily in conversation. I don't think I could study alone.'

He went to the shelf, picked out half a dozen volumes of the visitor's books and carried them to the table.

'It might be worth your while to look through the account books yourself,' she said.

'The accounts?' Wagstaff looked puzzled.

'To see if there is any unusual expenditure recorded at around the time of the deaths.'

'What sort of thing?'

'I'm not sure. Just anything unusual. A good set of accounts is an excellent historical record. Was your predecessor a good record-keeper?'

'Mr Warren was meticulous in every way, Miss Carew. He often told me I would find everything I needed to know in the accounts.'

'Well, then they are worth a half-hour's scrutiny too, I imagine.'

. . .

STARTING with the year she calculated Wagstaff was ten, Vita flicked through the pages of Crowswood's visitor's book. Visitors came, left, and wrote their thanks and their jovial messages to the host in large numbers, but judging by the dates they appended to their signatures, there were also long periods between gatherings at Crowswood, presumably when Mountfitchet was away in London. A few names–often boyish nicknames in wildly scribbled signatures–appeared repeatedly. *Fine shoot. Better luck next time, Bozzo.* Or *Enjoyable as ever, Digger.* By the end of the year, the pages were filled up with dashed-off signatures. *Again soon! Alessandra. Such dancing! Fi and Vivvy.*

Pages and pages of names, each a guest departing. What a different place Crowswood must have been, Vita thought, full of music and dinners, sport, and jolly entertainment. But then, among the flourishes and nicknames, one caught her eye. It was a neat message in old-fashioned handwriting: *A la prochaine fois, Mimi Joubert.* It stood out for being written in French, but also because the writer had incorporated a little bird in the signature–a quick little sketch–but recognisably a kingfisher.

'There! I think we have her,' Vita said.

Wagstaff stood and looked at the signature over her shoulder. She heard him draw a ragged breath, and did not turn to look, but guessed from the sound that he was in tears.

At that moment, Maria entered at the far end of the library and came over to them. She looked concerned when she saw Wagstaff, looking curiously at him. 'The doctor looks for you,' she told Vita. 'I take you.'

CHAPTER 23

'I imagine you will be glad to return to the peace and normality of Cambridge life, Miss Carew,' Dr Haslam remarked, folding his stethoscope and placing it in his bag. He took out a tongue depressor. The sight of it brought some of the horrors of earlier examinations back to his patient. She shuddered, but then opened her mouth resolutely for him to peer at her healing tonsils.

'All well. Coming on nicely,' he said. 'And the voice is normal?'

'Quite normal, I think,' she told him.

'You should have stayed silent for longer, but it seems you have done yourself no harm this time.' He washed his hands at the nightstand.

'May I ask you about Dr Bennett?'

'Bennett? I don't know a Bennett.' Haslam said.

'Are you sure?'

He looked at her sternly. Of course he was sure.

'But there was a Dr Bennett. I saw him several times. He was here at night.'

Haslam closed his bag with a click and picked it up. 'You were delirious for several days and nights. Dr Bennett sounds to me like a figment of your feverish imagination. Was he agreeable?'

'He seemed kind, but overworked.'

'Well, that has the ring of truth about it, but there is no Dr Bennett practicing in this area, I can assure you.'

He straightened his back and said rather sharply, 'This being Crowswood Castle, I expect you want me to say there once was a Dr Bennett, but he died tragically and his ghostly spirit has been visiting patients for the last hundred years to compensate for his earthly career being cut off in its prime, or some such nonsense.'

'No, I...'

'Well, that is the kind of thing the servants enjoy telling visitors, but it isn't true. There's no nice young Dr Bennett. He didn't visit you. You were just feverish and seeing visions. The only doctor who has treated you is me, dull old flesh-and-blood Dr Haslam. And I have made rather a good job of those tonsils.'

'You have. I apologise. Thank you Dr Haslam. Thank you very much.'

'I agree with your aunt, by the way, that overwork

can be damaging to the health. As well as making terrible patients, medical people are prone to overwork. It is best avoided. One needs to regulate oneself and guard against it. It does no good in the long run.'

'Do you avoid overwork yourself, Doctor?' Vita asked.

Haslam smiled and said, 'Not always, but I have a charming wife and three dear and very insistent children, which helps.'

He nodded, picked up his bag, then added without looking at his patient, 'I re-sat several examinations during my studies. Most of us did. Medicine is a hard life. It is not for everyone, but you shouldn't let a single failed examination stop you,' before leaving the room.

THE DOCTOR's remark still hung in the air when Maria knocked and invited Vita to join the ladies downstairs.

Vita followed the maid along yet more of the labyrinthine corridors of the castle into the redecorated area she had seen on arrival at Crowswood. What an age ago that seemed! She found her aunt and Miss Navarro in the large sitting room by the fire.

'What a pleasure to see you well and out of bed, Miss Carew,' Consuela Navarro said. 'Your aunt and I were discussing how all this is to be managed.'

'How all what is to be managed?' Vita asked, taking a seat on the sofa next to her aunt.

'The dead bodies and so forth,' Miss Navarro said. She wore a look of irritated distaste, as if corpses were an inconvenience roughly similar to an error in the wine order.

'One has already been removed by the coroner's officer, I believe,' Vita said, 'but that was partial, we now know, so he will have to come back for the other arm…'

She was interrupted by a delicate cough and looked up to see both the other ladies looking appalled. '… I apologise, I forget I am more used to such things than most. I did not phrase that very delicately. He will have to retrieve the remains of those remains, so to speak. And then there is the female corpse we discovered in the back of the icehouse.'

'Oh, good heavens!' her aunt said. 'Who is that poor creature? Do we know?'

'We think it is a lady called Mimi Joubert, who was killed by the Earl when he threw her down the stairs.'

Consuela crossed herself. 'Yes. Wagstaff saw it as a little boy. He told me,' she said. 'All his life he kept it secret.'

'And he told you about locking the icehouse gate too?'

'He did.' Miss Navarro nodded.

'Have I missed something?' Louisa asked. 'I don't understand.'

'Wagstaff told both of us that as a child he had seen a dead woman in the blue dress lying at the foot of the stairs one morning. He also saw the Earl move the body, but he did not know what happened to it after that. He was too young to know what to do. He never dared to speak of it. Then some time later, the old butler asked him to do one thing–lock the old ice house gate. If he did this, he would be kept safe at Crowswood and be able to work here and make it his home. He was an orphan from the workhouse,' Vita added. 'So a safe home was something he longed for.'

'And he did as he was asked?' said her aunt.

Consuela and Vita both nodded.

'And nobody ever mentioned what had happened again?' Louisa looked from Consuela to Vita in astonishment.

'No, apparently not,' Vita said. 'When the workmen found the body, Wagstaff immediately thought it must be this lady in blue. He guessed that the Earl had hidden her there. He was relieved. What had happened to her body was a mystery that had haunted him. But when I examined the body the workmen found, it wasn't a woman's body. It was a man's.'

'You can tell that?' her aunt said.

'Yes, there are easily discernible differences. But the body was incomplete. An arm had become

179

detached. The workmen dug the remains up hurriedly and left the right arm behind.'

Her aunt looked appalled.

'I went to the ice house with Wagstaff to find the missing limb. We did so easily enough. We also came across the crow signet ring the Earl always wore. It is absolutely distinctive.'

'So while the family lawyers scoured Europe for Mountfitchet, he was dead in the ice house all along?'

'It appears so, yes.'

'Did nobody think to look there before? Did no-one search the grounds?' Louisa asked.

'The ice house was not so easy to find. The entrance was overgrown. And, if we are to believe Wagstaff, the staff would obviously not encourage anyone to search there,' Consuela said.

'Even so,' Louisa shook her head, perplexed.

'People were convinced that the Earl had simply gone to one of his other homes. He had a place in France, and one in London. He came and went on a whim. He was often away,' Consuela told her.

'If he had been a popular man, well-loved and respected, the search might have been more thorough and efficient. Don't you agree?' Louisa said.

Consuela nodded. 'Yes. Nobody seems to have exerted themselves very much in the search. That is true. Not until the lawyers became involved and a great castle and its estate needed a new owner. At that point, agents keen to earn a fee began to scour the world for an heir. And eventually, they found me, a distant cousin who had never even heard of Crowswood, but whose great-grandfather left here almost a century earlier.'

'Had everyone forgotten Lady Caroline?' Louisa asked. 'She was locked away, but still living. Had she no claim to Crowswood?'

'She had been ruled insane and unfit. She had a claim, but only if she hired lawyers and made one. She did not do so. She wanted nothing to do with the place. She was happy where she was.'

'It is a litany of misery,' Louisa said sadly.

Miss Navarro rose and poured a glass of sherry for each of them, carrying them over on a tray.

'The other body was the lady in blue. Or, to be precise, it is the body of a young woman. The remains of her clothing and the single shoe we found with her seem once to have been bright blue.'

'So this is the lady Wagstaff had seen dead as a boy?'

Consuela nodded. They all sipped their sherry.

'It is for the police to look into all this, surely?' Louisa said.

'I shall send for them again, but they do not come quickly. Oh, this place! This Crowswood!' Miss Navarro made a gesture of dramatic resignation that seemed to Vita to be particularly South American.

'But the reputation of the place, the hauntings and

so on, have never concerned you in the past, I thought?' Vita said.

'No. I do not worry about these things. We have a different way of thinking about death and spirits and so on, where I come from. We do not fear them. They are an accepted part of our life. So here, in the castle, I was not worried. People die; their spirits are restless sometimes. It happens. Dead bodies and killings that have been kept secret for years–I was not expecting that, but I am a practical woman. I only need to know what to do about it. Then I can return to my horses.'

'As my aunt said, the rest is for the police,' Vita told her.

'Excellent! Then I shall send for them again immediately.' She stood to leave, but then turned. 'But, Miss Carew, I have another matter I should like to discuss. Maria, would you fetch Lady Caroline, please?'

She took Vita's hand. 'Vita, I have asked Lady Caroline to join us because she has expressed an interest in what I am going to say. As you know, she is an unusual person. She thinks in her own way, but I respect her ideas.

'Now, as you know, Miss Carew, I am a wealthy woman,' Miss Navarro said. 'I have been able to make my own choices in life. Coming here, for example. Bringing my horses. Inviting Lady Caroline to live in the cottage. She, too, has considerable means now.'

Lady Caroline came in and took a seat near the fire. She seemed to be holding a merry secret back, like a child who knows what's inside the present before it's unwrapped. Repressed excitement made her fidget with her gloves and keep re-arranging her skirts.

'Lady Caroline and I have discussed this,' Miss Navarro continued, 'and we have both decided that we would like to make you an offer.'

Vita had no idea what they meant. She looked from Consuela's dark features to Lady Caroline's pale face.

'Hee!' the older lady said, clapping her hands together.

'If you would permit it, we should like to…'

At that moment, the door was flung open and Wagstaff burst into the room carrying a large accounts ledger.

'I have it! I think I have it!' he said.

CHAPTER 24

*W*agstaff had bookmarked several places in the two account books he was carrying.

The first entry he pointed to itemised a payment of one guinea to G. Pinkney. '*For removal by cart at night*' on June 14th 1876.

There were several other payments in the following year to G. Pinkney, but none for as much as a guinea. The usual payment was two shillings '*for boys at night*'.

'I wondered why he paid a whole guinea for moving something by cart, when there were several carts in the yard,' Wagstaff told them. 'I knew already that Pinkney's boys were paid by the Earl to run about the castle at night and make noises. They banged doors and made howling and rustling noises in order to frighten the countess. The Earl paid them. Or rather, he ordered the butler to pay them. The butler entered the payment, as he would record any other transaction, in the accounts.'

'So the guinea fee was for…?' Consuela began.

'… for removing the lady in the blue dress. Presumably for taking her body and leaving it in the icehouse.'

Vita and Miss Navarro peered at the butler's neatly handwritten entry in the accounts in astonishment.

'We can't be sure of that,' Vita said. 'This Pinkney–whoever he was–might have been moving something else.'

'Why do it at night?' Louisa asked. 'And why pay this man when there were presumably plenty of other carts here waiting to be used? And gardeners who could do it without being paid a whole guinea?'

'He used Pinkney for his secret work, I'd guess,' Wagstaff said.

'Secret work such as hiding a poor woman's dead body!' cried Louisa.

'But why enter a secret payment in the account books at all?' Vita asked.

Wagstaff smiled. 'Mr Warren was a meticulous man. If he made a payment, he recorded it. He could not risk an error in his accounts. He would be held responsible himself, if one were found.'

'Do you remember this Pinkney?' Miss Navarro asked Wagstaff.

'I remember his boys. They gave me a good kicking whenever they came. One of them is the village blacksmith now.'

'And the father?' Vita asked.

'Dead at least a dozen years ago. In Norwich jail. Killed a man in a fight, if I remember rightly.'

Everyone looked again at the account books, struggling to take in the drama their tidy lines concealed.

BEFORE HE CONTINUED, Wagstaff spoke quietly to Miss Navarro, who nodded and rang for a maid.

'Lady Caroline needs a rest, Maria. Take her home and keep her company for a while, please,' she said.

Lady Caroline accepted this gracefully and was led away.

'Having found these entries in the ledger,' Wagstaff continued, 'I became curious. If one secret payment could be recorded, I thought there might be others, so I looked back into the accounts for ten years before, around the time of my birth. I found this.' He opened another of the great accounts ledgers and turned it so that the others could see. Among a list of payments for staff wages was one reading *Mary Wagstaff, wages in lieu of notice. Discharged.*

'She was a housemaid,' the butler said. 'She was discharged with five shillings.'

'Sent away?' Louisa asked. 'Do we know why?'

'I was born six months later,' Wagstaff said.

Everyone in the room turned to look at the butler in shock. 'I always wondered where my name came from. Foundlings left at the workhouse were allocated names by the wardens. There was a register, and they assigned names in alphabetical order. I always thought that was what happened with me, but it seems possible that my name might have come from this housemaid, Mary Wagstaff. She is, presumably, my mother.'

The ladies gasped.

'And your father?' Consuela asked, voicing the question everyone wanted to ask.

'Unknown,' Wagstaff said. 'It says so on the certificate they gave me. But if you look carefully at the entry about Mary Wagstaff, there is a note in the margin.'

They all examined the book again. After the word *discharged*, *see endpapers* had been written in smaller letters and different, paler ink.

'I also found this tucked into the binding of the book at the back.' Wagstaff showed them an envelope. 'It was concealed. Mr Warren always said I could find everything I needed in the accounts. This must be what he meant.'

'May I?' Vita asked. Wagstaff had paused for

some time, looking at the envelope. The hand he held it in was trembling, they noticed. He nodded and allowed Vita to take it and extract a letter.

The envelope was addressed to *Mr Warren, Butler to the Earl of Mountfitchet, Crowswood Castle, Norfolk*. The letter itself was on poor quality paper and written with a bad nib, much smudged and blotted, in loopy schoolgirl's handwriting.

> *The White Hart Inn,*
> *Seaton,*
> *Norfolk,*
> *July 18th 1866*

Dear Mr Warren,

I was delivered last Wednesday the 12th of a boy child they say will live. Being by myself and with no home or means, I had no choice but to leave the child to the care of the workhouse in Dereham.

I asked that he should keep my name of Wagstaff and have the first name of William. The matron said that since I was unwed and leaving him to the care of others I had no rights so I cannot say whether those names will stick. In truth sir, it broke my heart.

Mr Warren, you did what you could to help me in my time of trouble and I am thankful. I was happy in my work at Crowswood, but for the master and what he did to me. My cousin has given me work to tide me over for the next few weeks at the White Horse in

Seaton, for which I thank the Good Lord in Heaven.
After that time, I do not know what my future will be. I
weep for that, but I weep still more for my poor
little boy.

If Josiah Pickney, he that is prentiss to the smith,
should ask after me, please tell him I am well and no
longer in the difficult situation I found myself in
before.

Sincerely yours,
Mary Wagstaff

'THE MASTER and what he did to me,' Louisa
repeated, when the letter had been read aloud. 'She
implies that the Earl fathered her boy?'

'Yes. And that she was unwilling,' Wagstaff said.

The ladies looked at him, trying to gauge his reaction to this terrible information. Wagstaff astonished
them all by smiling.

CHAPTER 25

'So,' Consuela said, raising a glass to Wagstaff a little later, 'we are related!'

'Distantly related, but yes,' he said.

'And does this mean that you have a title? Are you the next Earl?' Louisa asked.

'I couldn't say. Lawyers must decide all that.'

'Crowswood might be yours!'

'Lady Caroline has rights to it, too, remember,' he said, 'as do you, Miss Navarro.'

'I shall invite Lady Caroline to join us for dinner. We can break this news to her then. She may not grasp the implications of this very quickly,' Miss Navarro said.

Louisa frowned. 'I hope it will not be too shocking for her. Her constitution is delicate.'

'She has survived a great many difficulties. It seems unlikely that she would be capsized by this.

She already knows and trusts you, Wagstaff–I should call you William now, I suppose.' Consuela was smiling.

'But speaking of being capsized by these revelations, your own reaction seems extraordinarily serene,' Louisa told him.

'I have always felt there was something hidden from me, something I needed to know. And now I have it. I understand why I was fetched from the workhouse when a new kitchen boy was needed. It was Warren's way of bringing me back to where he felt I belonged. He gave me a home here because he felt it was the natural order of things. He couldn't announce my identity to the world, but he could give me a home here at Crowswood.'

'But Warren also conspired with the others to involve you in killing Mountfitchet. Your own father,' Louisa said.

'We can't be absolutely sure of that,' Vita put in.

Her aunt shook her head. 'The old butler must have known. The servants would have known that the Earl had forced himself on poor Mary Wagstaff. They would have hated him for it. Still more when the child ended up in the workhouse.'

'You must wonder what became of your mother,' Consuela said. 'She might still be living. She was probably very young at the time.'

Wagstaff only smiled. Everyone looked curiously at him. He seemed to glow with a secret he could hardly contain, and finally said, 'I believe she lives in the village. She visits here twice a week. She married the apprentice blacksmith she mentioned in the letter. Mary Wagstaff became Mary Pinkney. She has baked pies and done the laundry here for as long as I can remember.'

'So the old butler did as she asked in the letter. He *did* remember her to Josiah Pinkney, the apprentice at the blacksmith's,' Vita said.

'He did, and Josiah–the only Pinkney in several generations to make an honest living–took up with Mary, despite everything. So you see, I have found a dead father, but I have also found a living mother who, as it turns out, has visited me almost every week of my life.'

'The answer was in the library all along,' Vita said.

'It was, but it took your fresh eyes to see it, Miss Carew.'

'It was just nosiness and idle curiosity,' Vita said.

'Then I propose a toast to nosiness and idle curiosity.'

And they all raised their glasses to salute those fine, but undervalued characteristics.

'I KNEW he was kind and brave because of my pony, Magnet.' Lady Caroline drifted into Vita's room the following morning.

Maria had thrown open the armoire and was packing Vita's clothes, having firmly refused Vita's suggestion that she might pack for herself.

'The Earl wanted Magnet sold to the Pinkneys. For dog meat, I imagine. Mountfitchet never liked Magnet. But before anyone could take him, Wagstaff —he was only a boy then—harnessed Magnet into the little cart and drove him over to me in Garston Lacey. I'll never forget it. He risked prison for horse theft to do that. Prison or worse—they might have transported him as a criminal. But he did that for me. Once I had my little horse, I could drive out again. I could have a life again. And when Consuela came to live here, it was he, Wagstaff, who told her about me. They closed the asylum at Garston Lacey. He asked her if I could come to the cottage. And she said yes out of the kindness of her heart. There are such people in the world, you must always remember that, Dear. It is a confusing place, but there are some surprisingly good people in it.'

Lady Caroline held a lace handkerchief to her eye for a moment before continuing. 'I would prefer—of course, you don't need to listen to my opinion—but I should nonetheless prefer it if you did not become a mad doctor. The mad doctors that I have met have mostly not been kind. I suppose you might be a kind one, and that would be good. So I wouldn't insist on it as a condition, I wouldn't dream of that. It is just a preference. You can ignore it, if you wish.'

Vita looked in confusion at Lady Caroline, who was wearing her usual long gloves and grey dress. She wondered if the older lady was perfectly in control of her thoughts.

'May I ask why you always wear grey, Lady Caroline?' she asked.

'It was the uniform at the asylum, to distinguish the mad ones from the others. I am mad, I am not ashamed of it, so I wear it still to show that I am on the side of the mad ones. I'm talking nonsense again, am I? Oh dear. Miss Navarro will explain. She asked me to bring you to her. Come. She will speak more plainly than I.'

The Countess rose and led Vita firmly out of the room. She guided her to Miss Navarro's rooms, before leaving them.

Consuela Navarro was at a desk in her private sitting room, a colourfully furnished room with several large horse paintings. 'Ah, Vita,' she said. 'I want to talk to you. Has the Countess said anything?'

'Not really. Only that she would rather I did not become a mad doctor.'

Consuela laughed and said, 'Well, that is understandable enough. I have spoken to Haslam about training in medicine. He trained in Edinburgh, and believes it far superior to other medical schools.

Perhaps you should go to Edinburgh instead of Cambridge?'

'I doubt they would have me,' Vita told her. 'And besides, Cambridge is important to me. I am fond of my college. I should like to stay. But at present, I doubt whether either Edinburgh or Cambridge will have me.'

'Why do you doubt it?'

'I failed an important examination.'

'But that is nothing. Haslam explained that. One simply re-takes such an examination. It is common to do so, he says.'

Vita looked helplessly at her hostess, whose manner was brisk and who was holding a pen in her hand. It appeared to hover over a half-written letter.

'It is not so simple. I have to convince the authorities that I am good enough to pursue medicine, and so far I have not performed particularly well.'

Miss Navarro replaced the cap on her pen and laid it on the desk. 'Vita, I should like to offer you some advice. You will permit me to do so?'

'Of course,' Vita said, bracing herself for what was to come.

'You must be braver, Vita. Bolder.'

'Ah,' Vita said.

'Come with me. I think more clearly out of doors.' Consuela strode out of the room. Vita had to scurry to keep up.

Pausing only to equip themselves with coats and

hats, which Consuela provided from a large store, they ventured out, crossed the yard, and followed the path to the stables.

Vita had never seen the place in daylight. It was an expansive cobbled square with stabling on three sides and a sizeable well in the centre. They entered through a broad archway surmounted by a clock tower.

Consuela paused in the gateway to admire her domain. 'Beautiful, no?' she said.

The place was a hive of activity. Horses being groomed, fed, led out for schooling in the fields. Someone was sweeping the immaculate yard. Rows of horses were looking over their stable doors. They greeted their mistress by nodding their heads and snorting. Consuela led Vita over to the first horse box.

'When I was nine years old, I told my parents I would never marry,' she said, greeting the glossy black horse by rubbing its ears. 'I said they were not to expect it. I would train horses instead, and breed the finest in Argentina. At nine years old, I made this choice.'

'And they accepted your decision?'

'Of course. Everybody accepted it. It was only much later that I realised not everybody has my luck, or my strength of purpose. I was born with it. In my cradle, I was determined to have my own way, but many girls are not like me. You, I think, are easily filled with doubt. Am I right about this?'

'I suppose so,' Vita said.

'So you must learn to stand up for yourself. When they try to stop you, you should argue with them. Stand your ground! Refuse to let them put fear or self-doubt into your mind. I have noticed that English women,' she moved to the next horse, a glossy chestnut, and stroked the white star on its forehead, 'English woman lack a certain healthy pride that we women from Argentina are given by nature. Do you agree?'

Vita had no time to reply because Consuela continued, 'We Argentinian women have a natural sense of our own worth, our own powers. It is a spirit we are born with. English women are – you will excuse me – they are apologetic!'

She opened the stable door and stepped inside to look the horse over more closely, running her hand down each of its legs and over its back. It flicked its long tail.

'Your aunt,' Consuela continued, moving on to the next horse box, 'she is not like that. She is an artist and knows how good she is. That's why we are friends. Louisa told me that your father will re-marry and cannot pay for your studies. He wishes you to stay at home in – where is the place?'

'Devon,' Vita said.

'Yes. A far-away place without medical schools. Is that correct?'

'It is.'

'So, Vita, this is what will happen. You will allow me to pay for your college expenses, all of them, until you are a qualified doctor. How long does it take to finish all those examinations?'

Vita was left blinking. Consuela patted the neck of the next horse and straightened the net of hay it was eating from.

'How long?' Consuela repeated.

'Four years more, at least. It might even be five.' Vita winced as she said it.

Consuela dismissed this with a sweep of her hand. 'See! You apologise! You should stop this. As long as you need; I pay.'

Vita was left speechless and rooted to the spot as her hostess turned abruptly to discuss something with one of the red-hatted gaucho trainers who was leading a grey pony past.

The mare, Esperanza, was in the next box with her foal. The mother made a whickering sound of greeting to Consuela as they approached, and the foal looked over curiously. He was a handsome little creature, darker than his mother, with a black mane and stumpy black tail.

Vita leaned over the stable door. 'I'm sorry, but I cannot accept such an offer,' she said. 'It is far too generous.'

Consuela went into the loose box with the horses, patting Esperanza and holding her hand out to the foal, who hid behind his mother. She directed her answer to the mare, as if it were Esperanza who needed a scholarship fund. 'Allow me to do this. It would make me happy. Do it to please me. It is a simple thing. Say yes and go back to your books. All that studying! It is a life I should hate, but if it is what you want, then, Vita, do it! And stop apologising!'

The mare turned her head and looked at Vita. The foal did the same. All three of the occupants of the stable paused and looked at her with dark, expectant eyes.

It suddenly felt priggish and surly to refuse.

VITA WALKED the chilly path back from the stables alone, feeling the sky had lifted and everything had brightened around her. The wintery sun seemed warmer, the trees full of the promise of new leaf. By the time she reached the castle, her face ached with smiling, but there were tears in her eyes as well.

So now, all that remained was the small matter of persuading her father, Newton college and the university authorities that she was capable. Every bit of the confidence Miss Navarro advised would be needed, but striding at that moment through the cold, bright air, Vita felt certain it was worth a try.

CHAPTER 26

'*L*ook,' her aunt said, looking out of the window of her room a little later. Vita stood beside her and both watched from two storeys up as a plain horse and cart drove into the service yard.

'What is it?' Vita asked.

'I think this lady is Mrs Pinkney, Wagstaff's mother. The one who wrote the letter all those years ago. She is bringing the clean laundry. I wonder whether he'll speak to her about his discovery.'

'Aunt! Is it proper of us to spy on them at such a moment?'

The pressed themselves against the walls on either side, so as not to be too obvious from below.

'It is not spying. We just happened to be looking out of the window. I wouldn't dream of spying! Oh, Vita, look! There is Wagstaff approaching.'

The butler, formal in his overcoat, walked over to the cart and lifted a large linen sack down. Mrs Pinkney reached and handed him a small basket of provisions. They appeared to exchange pleasantries.

'How will the poor woman react, if Wagstaff suddenly declares himself her son?' Vita said. 'It might come as a terrible shock.'

From that distance, they could see Mrs Pinkney nodding as if agreeing that the weather was, indeed, rather chilly, but then there came a moment where the butler stepped closer to her, looked up into her face and said something else. As he did this, he reached and took hold of one of her mittened hands, which was clasping the horse's reins.

Vita and Aunt Louisa saw Mrs Pinkney put the fingers of her other hand to her mouth, her forehead, her mouth again. She seemed about to fall forward, so Wagstaff had to help her step down off the cart and steady her as she stood beside it, leaning against the wheel. She was a short, round woman with wisps of hair flying out from her bonnet and a shawl tightly tied around her. There was one more moment of hesitation, with Wagstaff looking at her anxiously, but then she raised her head to look up at him, threw open her arms and pulled her lost son into a long embrace, which he returned.

Their joy was clear from two floors above.

'Oh,' Louisa said, with a slight sniff, 'that was a

more touching scene than I had expected. I am glad to see them united.'

'The odd thing is that they were never really apart, except at the very beginning,' Vita reminded her. 'I wonder why she never told him he was her son?'

'There was terrible shame in her situation, remember,' Louisa said, 'however unjustly she was treated. I imagine she wanted to spare him that. And perhaps Mr Pinkney, the good blacksmith, did not know the whole story either.'

They both looked down into the yard again and watched as, arm in arm, Wagstaff and his mother stood talking.

THEY WERE in the stylish carriage, well wrapped by Maria in furs and rugs, and they had already said long goodbyes to Lady Caroline and Consuela Navarro, when Wagstaff appeared for a final time and handed them the package that contained the little kingfisher blue shoe.

'I should like this lady, Mimi, to have a funeral at last,' he said. 'My father, obviously, will be buried. But this Mimi, his victim, deserves to be treated decently. We know almost nothing about her. I already have a great deal to thank you for, but I wonder, Miss Carew, as one last favour, if you would take this, and see if you can find anything else about her?'

SO THE SHOE travelled back with them to Eden Street in Cambridge. And soon after, happy in the knowledge that Monsieur was preparing something delicious for dinner, and that whatever it was, it was almost certainly not beef, Vita asked the chef whether he had ever heard the name Mimi Joubert in the past. He had, after all, spent time in Paris in his youth.

'But of course! Mimi Joubert, she was well known,' he said. 'A singer. A famous beauty. She was on billboards. She was a big star.'

Did he know what had become of her?

The chef answered this with a grand Gallic shrug. 'Swept off her feet by some wealthy gentleman, I imagine,' he said. 'They burned bright, the stars in those days, but their fame did not last long.'

'How can I find out more about her?' Vita asked.

The chef was piping cream onto a row of delicate pastries.

'For that you will have to go to Paris.'

OVER DINNER, Vita said, 'I shall need to speak to my father, Aunt, about Miss Navarro's willingness to pay my university expenses. Will it be difficult for him to accept her offer, do you think?'

'We can discuss that on the boat train, Dear,' her aunt replied, taking a sip of the cider Monsieur had brought back from Normandy. 'I suggest we go quite soon. I haven't seen Paris for years!'

IF YOU ENJOYED this Vita Carew mystery, there are other titles you might like:

Poison at Pemberton Hall
A Thin Sharp Blade
Dr Potter's Private Practice
The Painted Penny Stamp

A QUICK RATING or review is a great way to help other readers find the series.

AUTHOR'S NOTE

The starting point for this story was reading about Victorian 'mad doctors' and asylums. The specialism of psychiatry was in its infancy at that time, and the understanding of mental illness very limited, but there was money to be made by running remote asylums for rich families who needed problematic relations housed. I imagined Garston Lacey, Lady Caroline's asylum, as rather a pleasant place. Some asylums were genuine sanctuaries offering peaceful surroundings, but many were run along harsh, and even cruel lines.

The Married Women's Property Act*, allowed married women in England to own and control property in their own right for the first time. Until then, all land and property owned by a woman became her husband's on marriage, and she had no control over it.

There were a number of court cases around this

time, where a husband who wanted to gain control of a wealthy wife's fortune tried to have her declared insane and committed to an asylum. Since there was no recognised definition of insanity, it was extremely difficult to prove whether someone was insane or sane. Court cases ran for years, with family members and household spies reporting on the woman's behaviour and long debates over the exact point at which eccentricity (in one case, inviting a whole circus with all its performers and animals to come and live in the family's smart London townhouse) shaded into madness.

All this was hard to resist. So I imagined a case, where a dreadful Earl set about driving his already delicate wife mad by frightening her out of her wits in the perfect setting of a haunted and gloomy castle. The castle is loosely based on Audley End House near Saffron Walden in Essex. Audley End is not a castle at all, but a huge Tudor house. When it was built as a private home by a government official, it was so grand that even King Henry VIII considered it excessive. It's open to visitors now, and not as creepy as the made-up Crowswood Castle, at least not in daylight, but it does have a large collection of taxidermy animals and birds. They were the treasured collection of an enthusiastic naturalist, but it's hard for a present day visitor to look at them without a shudder.

I recommend a visit.

Fran Smith

January 2023

Legal experts will spot that the Married Women's Property Act was passed in 1882, too late for my story. I used my authorial powers under the Poetic Licence Act of 2023 to pretend it was already in force.